SUFFER THE CHILDREN

THE GHOSTS OF REDRISE HOUSE

CAROLINE CLARK

CAZCLARK.COM

THE GHOSTS OF REDRISE HOUSE

This is a three book series that that tells the story of the spirit Old Hag. Each book can be read alone but I think you will enjoy them more if you read them in order. The first two books are on **SALE** for **0.99** for a limited time.

Book 1: The Ghosts of RedRise House – The Sacrifice

Book 2: The Ghosts of RedRise House – The Battle Inside

Book 3 The Ghosts of RedRise House – Suffer the Children

* * *

The Ghosts of RedRise House Book 1 - The Sacrifice

Rosie is running from her past. Looking for peace and a new beginning. House sitting in the luxurious and romantic RedRise House seemed like a perfect plan to rediscover herself and rebuild her life.

It is so far away from the past that she knows she can look to the future and yet something is not quite right. She hears voices, footsteps in the night. She wakes from terrible nightmares. Strange figures stare down at her bed with hidden faces — was it all just a dream?

Then there are the ghostly children. Are they all part of her imagination or did something terrible happen here?

Like animals, the children fight for her blood. Will they get it or is something darker waiting and watching for its chance to escape?

Find out if Rosie will ever leave RedRise house or if she will join the children to stay in this haunted house for all time. The Ghosts of RedRise House – The Sacrifice on SALE for just 0.99 for a limited time and FREE on Kindle Unlimited.

* * *

The Ghosts of RedRise House Book 2 – The Battle Within

The Ghosts of RedRise House have escaped. Something evil is stalking the city and only Rosie stands between it and a chain of misery and death.

Having escaped the haunted RedRise House with her life Rosie begins to wonder if she escaped with her sanity. She is hearing voices, seeing strange things, and waking up covered in blood. What did she bring back with her?

The voice in her head wants to kill her friend. Can Rosie survive long enough to find out what is wrong? Can she regain control and beat so ancient a spirit?

Biding her time she must be clever. Must use her knowledge of the world and find help but will it be enough?

The race is on and the price for losing is more than she can bear.

Find out if Rosie can survive in The Ghosts of RedRise House - The Battle Within – on SALE for just 0.99 for a limited time and FREE on Kindle Unlimited.

Get a FREE short story and never miss a book. Subscribe to Caroline Clark's newsletter for new release announcements and occasional free content: http://eepurl.com/cGdNvX

edRise House
Yorkshire Moors

England.

10 p.m.

Sprinting through a dark and clouded night, a young boy raced as if for his life. Tiny bare feet made no sound as he tore along an overgrown path. So thin, so frail, and yet he raced like the devil was on his tail. Arms pumping, lips pulled back into a snarl. The breeze didn't lift his home-cut hair as step by step he ran on and on.

Though weeds and brambles blocked his path, he passed through them without hinder as he ran toward the freedom of the countryside beyond.

Behind him, a chill, keening sound started. Stood at the door of a once imposing house were over a dozen children. None of whom moved their mouths, yet the sound came from them and rose upon the air. Louder and louder, higher and higher. Like nails on a chalkboard, it shattered the stillness and ripped through the quiet. Was it encouragement, disapproval or despair? It followed him, as step by step he came closer to freedom. Closer to the open grassland dotted with trees, and beyond that the world.

Yet the shadow of the hulking house stretched out into the darkness, and he had yet to break its reach.

It had once been an impressive sight, but now the front door hung half open. Broken windows winked in the black night and yet kept the secrets within. A tile had slipped from the roof and lay shattered on the path. Weeds crowded the garden. Straggly, forest-like growths had attempted to take over, but instead, lay brown and dying around the base of the house and the front door.

Surrounding that door were over a dozen children, ranging from five to twelve years in age. Although it was difficult to tell, for all of them were small and malnourished. They wore old-fashioned clothes. The girls dressed in plain, dark, work dresses that came down to their bare feet. The material patched and threadbare in places. The boys' trousers didn't quite cover their bony ankles and were topped with plain dark smocks.

Despite the late hour and the chill of the night, they didn't shiver... they simply stood looking, staring as if at freedom. Their big eyes, white against dirty skin, pleaded for escape. On either side of them, standing like a sentinel, were adult figures. Cloaked in long dark robes that covered their heads and hid their features. One was smaller, perhaps a woman, but it was impossible to tell.

The keening hit a note so high it must surely shatter the houses remaining windows. The boy was so close to escaping… just five more feet and he would clear the house grounds, clear the shadow. He would be free of the jungle of weeds and place his bare feet on the rolling grasslands.

At the door, the children shuffled on the spot… leaning forward as if to push him those last few paces. Their faces were lit with excitement, hope, and yet beneath it all, was the mask of fear. This was false hope, and they knew it.

One more step and the boy was gone. The keening was replaced by a collective sigh of disappointment. They stepped back, making room, and were not surprised when the ginger-headed child appeared before them. Tears ran down his cheeks, tracing a clean path through the dirt.

The children all crowded around him offering support though none tried to touch him. They knew better.

Then one by one they threw back their heads, and the keening rose into the night. It was a sound so terrible… it told of their pain and their eternal torment. Now, it was clear why they didn't move their lips; the sound came from the brutal slashes across their throats. The torn and bloodied skin flapped as the noise rose into the night.

The adults remained still, like statues, and yet despair came from them too. This was not a good place, not a place that they intended to stay.

* * *

LEEDS MAGISTRATE COURT

Westgate

Leeds

West Yorkshire

LS1 3BY

1:30 pm

PERCHED on the edge of the hard bench, Shelly waited for the twelve people to file back into the room and take their seats. It was hard to keep still, hard not to smile, but she knew it was inappropriate. A hand took hers and squeezed it gently.

Looking up she nodded at Jack. A similar light lit his sea blue eyes as she knew shone in her brown ones. There was the touch of stubble on his chin. How long had it been since they had gone home? Three weeks. Three exciting weeks they had sat here. Waiting, hoping, wanting to hear the details of what had happened. Though they knew what they heard would be but a faint impression of the truth. The truth was too much for this courtroom. It was up to them to find it. To prove it. To free Miss Benson.

Shelly's mousy brown ponytail swished through the air as she turned to glance around the courtroom. Leaning forward, she licked her lips as the jurors sat down, leaving just the foreman standing. Breath held she waited, wanting justice, but fearing it was as elusive as the ghosts she so wanted to find.

The courtroom was full and had been so for most of the trial, but today the mood was different. For so long it had been depressing, painful almost, to see the faces ravaged with pain and grief. Today there was anticipation. It buzzed and clung in the air. It was reflected in the stiff shoulders, the shiny eyes, and the way that some of the relatives perched on the edge of their seats. Just like Shelly, they waited for justice. Licking lips, tasting it in the air, but fearing they wouldn't get it.

Some of the family members had stared at them at first. Their blank eyes accusing, asking. *Why are you here?* It didn't bother Shelly.

What they did was unconventional, there would always be those who didn't understand. That was part of the job, she knew it, and she knew this was their job to do. Their time. It was harder to comprehend why Jesse and Gail had abandoned Rosie Benson. Why they refused to tell the court what had *really* happened. It felt like a betrayal and had angered her at first. Only now did she see it as an opportunity. The two ghost hunters simply watched the trial with Amy Firth. Merely consoling her or giving Rosie a nod or a supportive glance.

What use was that?

They were supposed to be heroes. Supposed to be real paranormal investigators and yet their client was here, standing trial for murder.

Shelly knew she would never let this happen to a client of hers. She would get them off no matter what it took. Pulling her eyes from the two investigators, she turned back to the court.

Rosie sat just in front and to the left of them, waiting for the verdict to be read out. She was thin, and dark lines marred her eyes, yet there was a sense of peace about her.

Shelly understood. Rosie had seen the truth. She knew there was more than this mundane world. She knew there was something after. That knowledge changed you. It had changed Shelly and Jack. It had given them a purpose. Now, this had happened in their town... a haunting, a possession, and the house it all started in was so close. Though they were both supposed to be at university, they had taken time off to watch this trial.

Paranormal studies hadn't taught her anything, anyway, and Jack was studying computer science. He was a genius at that sort of thing. Could teach his lecturers a thing or two. Missing a few weeks wouldn't matter too much. Not for something this important.

So every day they sat in the courtroom and listened to the evidence. Then they went back to the hotel and tried to work out what really happened. It was intriguing, exciting, and at the same time, frustrating having to read between the lines. What they wanted was a real haunting. All the details. What they wanted was something to fight, rights to wrong, evil to banish.

The clerk cleared his throat, and Shelly stilled her mind to listen. What verdict was given would impact on her future. On how easy it would be to help Rosie, on if they could even visit her.

If she were convicted of first-degree murder, then it would be unlikely that they would be allowed, at least not straight away. Holding her breath, she waited. Hopeful that this would go her way. That there would be a chance to help Rosie, to set her free, and to help all these grieving relatives. She wanted it so much and yet, like the relatives, she feared it wouldn't happen. Feared that Rosie would be locked up in a maximum security prison. One she wouldn't be granted access to.

Coming to his feet the clerk of the court faced the jury. "Will the jury please rise." He turned to Rosie. "Will the defendant also please rise and face the jury."

Wood scraped on the hard floor and the sound of people

standing echoed around the cavernous room. Shelly watched Rosie try to stand and wobble. The lawyer, Mr. Paul Simmons, put his hand under her elbow and helped her to her feet.

"Mr. Foreman, has your jury agreed upon your verdicts?"

A kindly man of about fifty looked down at the envelope in his hand. "We have." With a shaky hand, he passed the envelope to the clerk who took it to the judge. Silence was a beast waiting to pounce. It would change their future, she knew it. Anticipation stilled her breath.

"What say you, Mr. Forman, as to complaint number 5879643, wherein the defendant is charged with three counts of first-degree murder? Is she guilty or not guilty?"

The Foreman turned toward Rosie, and she wavered slightly. He looked down as if he couldn't face giving her such bad news.

Shelly almost let out a moan.

"Not guilty."

Had he really said that? Had she just wanted to hear it, just imagined it? She looked at Jack, he nodded. Shelly let out a small grunt of joy and felt a few disapproving eyes turn upon her. The relatives wanted Rosie to hang — they didn't understand. Shelly would help them see the truth.

"Order," the judge called as a murmur of dissent rumbled around the courtroom. "Order, order," his voice boomed across the rumblings, and the noise stopped.

The next charge had to be guilty, the solicitor had tackled this case by ignoring the truth. It angered Shelly and Jack too. This was a place where they should be able, to tell the truth. If they had, then Rosie would be a hero. She would be freed and thanked by the relatives. Instead, she would be shamed and locked up. The unfairness of it caused acid to rise in her throat and her heart burned with exasperation.

Rosie swayed a little and was steadied by her lawyer.

"What say you, Mr. Forman, as to complaint number 5879644, wherein the defendant is charged with three counts of manslaughter on the grounds of diminished responsibility? Is she guilty or not guilty?"

"Guilty."

Shelly let out a blast of disappointment, but she could hear mumbles of approval from the relatives. They felt they had received their pound of flesh. To them, it was over. They could mourn their dead and continue with their lives. Shelly intended to change that. With Jack, she would prove what had really happened and then she would visit the relatives and let them know that their loved ones had moved on. That there was something after. Then they would all join together to campaign to free Rosie.

Shelly watched as Rosie sank down into her seat. Amy approached her and pulled her into her arms. They hugged and were talking. Gail and Jesse hovered and exchanged words with the solicitor. As two guards waited ready to lead Rosie away.

Shelly wanted to rush up. To tell Rosie to hold on and she stood.

Jack grabbed her arm and pulled her back. "Not now," he said. "This is not the place."

"Yes, but I should tell her. She needs to know that someone cares." Frustration and excitement made her hands rise like birds ready for flight, but she knew that Jack was right. Though she wanted to run over there and tell Rosie what she had planned it was not the time. Now they would have to be patient. Raising her eyebrows, she gave Jack her cutest smile.

A big grin spread across his face. "Let's eat," he said and held out his arm.

Shelly took it and let him lead her from the courtroom. Suddenly she was starving and knew that they would visit the fried chicken restaurant next door. Despite her petite size, they would eat the biggest bucket there, she would eat the most. Twice as much as the 6 foot 2 inches of muscle that she called her friend. Together they would talk late into the night. A strategy had to be made, a plan devised, soon they would find out the truth.

CHAPTER 1

"*N*o."

Shelly felt as if she had been slapped and drew back from Rosie. *No,* how could she say no?

Across the light oak table, Rosie smiled. It was a look of peace, of understanding, fitting for this light, airy room. It had taken Shelly completely by surprise, even more, than the room had. Instead of bars and walls of glass between her and the inmates, there were tables, chairs, teal blue sofas and woodland murals on the walls. The room was full of patients and visitors, and yet it was quiet, relaxed, more like a spa than a high-security unit for the criminally insane.

That smile, the word no, it was the exact opposite of what Shelly expected. Right now she wanted to jump up and slap Rosie. To tell her there was hope but she couldn't. Beside her, Jack leaned forward and then sat back. The look on his face was as confused as Shelly's.

It had taken them two months to get here. Two long months of letters, phone calls, and research. At first, Rosie had flatly refused to see them. All along Jack had encouraged her in his own way. Telling her that Rosie would be confused, frightened, and maybe even still possessed.

"Perhaps the spirit wasn't exorcised?" he had said. "Perhaps we need to get into that hospital and save her from it."

Now those words came back to Shelly, and she stared at Rosie. Could it be true? In her bag, she had brought Holy Water, a cross and a Bible but these had all been confiscated. How would she find out if this woman before her, the one with the serene smile, was in fact possessed?

Part of her thought that must be the answer and her mouth opened and closed as she tried to think of a way to prove it. Of some clever words that would trick the spirit into revealing itself.

Jack beat her to it. "You are she," he said standing and pointing. Though his arm shook a little his words were said with confidence. "You're the Old Hag, the evil one and you will not beat us."

Shelly stood up next to him. "Don't give in Rosie we will find a way to save you."

Rosie smiled again. "I can assure you the spirit is gone. I understand your passion and your need to help, but there is nothing you can do. My body committed those crimes even if my mind didn't. People died because of these hands." Rosie held her hands up before her and Jack jumped in front of Shelly, raising his own arms as if he wished to fight.

"Relax," Rosie said. "I'm no threat. I'm free and I'm happy to stay here for as long as needed. Talk to Gail and Jesse, they will explain."

Shelly sat down and grabbed hold of Jack's suit jacket. It was a brown check, and it had buzzed her that he had worn it. It made him look so professional, and here she was in jeans and a t-shirt. Maybe that was why Rosie wasn't taking them seriously. Or maybe she had to say this. Maybe she was hiding her true feelings from the people who were guarding her.

Shelly winked and looked around the room. No one appeared to be watching, but that would be how they wanted it to look. "I understand. We will go to RedRise House and find out what we need to know. You sit tight... do what you need..."

"No!" Rosie shouted. "Stay away from there."

An orderly appeared as if out of nowhere, and Rosie lowered her voice. "Gail and Jesse will visit the house when the time is right, — you must stay away."

The orderly was gone, and so was Shelly's dream.

Jack put a hand on her shoulder, and she jumped and let out a little shriek. "Sorry," she said and gave him a smile.

He winked and turned to Rosie. Sitting back down. "We understand. We will leave this to the experts..."

What was he saying? Shelly wanted to tell him to stop, but her brain couldn't cope, and once more her mouth flapped in the wind.

"Maybe you would share your story with us," Jack continued. "The real story?"

Rosie let out a sigh. "If that will keep you from looking into this then yes I will. But promise me you will stay away from RedRise House."

"Yes of course," Shelly said for she understood what Jack was doing. Right at that moment, she wanted to hug him. To pull him into her arms and kiss his handsome lips. Only that would break their unwritten rule. They were friends, only friends. *Would he ever see that she wanted more?*

* * *

IT WAS two hours later that they left the secure unit with copious notes and more excitement than they could contain.

"You want to eat?" Jack asked as they climbed back into his nine-year-old Clio.

"Always."

"I thought so." He winked before turning the key. The engine turned over slowly and coughed like an asthmatic pig. Chug, chug, chug, at last, it fired, and Jack breathed a sigh of relief before turning the wheel out of the car park. "We passed some services a few miles back down the road."

Shelly nodded. She remembered seeing them on the way here. They had a lot to think about and drove in silence, but it was never uncomfortable. Shelly clutched onto the notes as if she feared that they could disappear just as easily as the spirits in Rosie's tale.

Once they were sat in the services, Jack with a coffee and a slice of toast and her with the mega all-day breakfast, they began to talk. The notes were open in front of them.

"What do you think?" Jack asked.

"That you are just the cleverest, most devious, and wonderful man that I know."

"Well yes!" he said, as a rose blush crept up his cheeks.

Shelly picked up a sausage on her fork and began to nibble at the delicious pork. Jack shifted uncomfortably in his seat knowing that she was unaware of the effect she had on him. Taking a sip of tea, he pulled his eyes back to the notes. "Are we going to see Gail and Jesse? Do you think they would... see us?"

Shelly finished the sausage and wolfed down her toast. Wiping her lips, she shook her head from side to side as if trying to decide on what to say. "Don't you dare think, that we are a waste of their time! I've seen things, know things, and you have researched and read up on this with me. We are as much experts as they were, are. I'm even taking the same course as Jesse, damn it."

Jack's eyes widened. "Yes, yes, we are quite the experts." Sitting up straight in the chair he smiled again. "So what's our next move, expert?"

"More toast and then we make a plan. I don't think we even bother going to see Gail and Jesse the so called Spirit Guides — I think we go straight to RedRise House and release those children."

Jack gulped and reached for his tie. Moving it away from his throat as if it were suddenly throttling him. "I say, do you really think we should do that?"

"Why not?" Shelly asked, but she loved his accent. So proper, so unlike her own. "We have the notes from Rosie, we have our Holy Water and our cross. We can do this."

Jack said nothing for a few moments, and she knew he wanted to bring Gail and Jesse with them. Part of him didn't believe her, but another part did. It was that part that was afraid, and yet she knew he would never say so. He would think and sometimes stutter but he would back her, and he would be there if she needed him.

"Do we just drive up to the house and break-in?" Jack asked as his Adam's apple bounced over his tie.

"We don't need to." Shelly's eyes widened as another plate of toast was dropped in front of her. She licked her lips. "I've been doing some research and the couple who own the house. An old retired couple called the Duncan's have agreed to meet us there."

Jack's eyes widened, and his mouth opened and closed. Shelly knew it was best to let him take his time and come to terms with how bold she had been. Taking her eyes off his rugged face, she slathered butter onto the toast and then popped a jar of jam. Before he could form a thought, she had topped the butter with jam and eaten half of the first round. It was delicious.

"When did you have in mind?" he asked.

"This next weekend is a bank holiday, and we have a full week off Uni. I thought we could travel up on Friday night and stay there the weekend and the following week. What d'ya say?"

"That soon... w... w... well yes why not."

"That's settled then." Shelly offered the plate over with the two remaining slices of toast and strawberry jam.

Jack shook his head. "I don't know where you put it. You're built like a stick insect, and yet you could eat for England."

"Oh! Thanks."

"No, I didn't mean that... you know you're beautiful."

Shelly felt heat hit her cheeks and she dropped her head allowing her ponytail to flick forward and hide a little of her blushes. How she wanted him to mean that. To really think that she was attractive, but they had been friends so long that she never believed he would see her as anything else... and yet... maybe this weekend could be romantic. How could she make it so?"

"Well, now I've stopped blushing we need to work out who pays what." Shelly waved her hand to indicate the plates on her side and the one on his.

"We split it down the middle just like always."

"But I got so much more than you. A full breakfast and three extra rounds of toast. You just had one toast and a black tea."

Jack laughed, it was a deep throaty sound, much more mature than anything she had heard from him before. Maybe they were both growing up. Though university was so perplexing that she felt like a kid at her first school once more. "I think you are just chivalrous. Are you sure?"

"I'm sure. Now, what do we need to plan for this trip?"

Shelly pushed her plate aside and clapped her hands. We will need to be prepared. I don't have any cold spot meters or EMF meters, but we can use cameras and our phones. We will need that book from the library."

"Book!"

"Oh yes, it lists a dozen or so exorcism's and different ways to communicate with the dead. I know we probably won't encounter anything, but just in case we need to be prepared."

"That sounds like a plan then. What about food and lodgings?"

17

Shelly smiled and felt a warmth rise up her chest. "I thought we could take sleeping bags. We can sleep on the floor or in any rooms that have furniture. Rosie said there was one bed." Heat raged across her cheeks.

Jack coughed. "You will have the bedroom of course."

"That is very gallant of you, but I think we should stick together. If these children are there and the adult spirits then we must be careful. They shouldn't be dangerous, not without Matron but who knows. We must take every precaution..."

"Yes, yes of course. I will stay by your side. I will guard you from any evil spirits."

"You are such a good friend." Why had she said that? "Having said all of this I think we should enjoy the time there. We can take some nice food and a bottle or two of wine."

"A beautiful house and a weekend away with a beautiful woman. That could be very romantic," Jack said.

"Yes, I'm sure it could." The look in his eyes filled her with joy. Maybe he was finally taking the hint and would realize that she wanted more. So why did she suddenly feel cold inside? Why did the hair raise on her arms? This was just an adventure. It wouldn't be dangerous.

CHAPTER 2

*J*ack steered the Clio carefully down the twisting country lanes and into a small village.

"There's a Chinese Takeaway," he called. "Get the number for later."

Shelly turned in her seat and tapped the number into her phone. Looking back over all their belongings, she wondered if they had brought everything they would need. For just a moment she was worried. *Were they up to this? What if there was still a malevolent spirit at the house? What would they do?*

"Are you worried?" Jack asked.

"Not at all. I was just trying to think whether we'd forgotten anything."

"I think we're gonna need a bigger car." He put on a Sheriff Broady accent.

"It's a boat." Shelly laughed. He was right though. The Clio was packed to bursting with everything they would need. There was nothing she couldn't handle, nothing they

19

couldn't handle. After all, she had seen a spirit before. Had spoken to it, had learned secrets from beyond the veil, and she would cope with this. A few desperate children needed her help. They would soon find out all about the children's lives. They would talk to them and learn from them, ask them to send a message. Then they would help them cross over. After that, she hoped that they would finally talk to each other about their personal lives.

This was her dream... a job. A getaway. A holiday with excitement, spirits, and hopefully romance. Who could ask for more?

The car left the village and zig-zagged across the moors for another twenty minutes. The poor headlights lit up little except the narrow, worn, and crumbling road as they traveled further from the village. Then in front of them a gateway loomed out of the darkness.

Two stone pillars were overgrown with brambles and ivy. They looked a little forlorn, and Shelly felt a moment of foreboding as they drove between them and onto the property.

The Duncans had told her to follow the drive for a mile and a half. It was like being in a country park. Rolling grassland was dotted with trees, but there were no animals or signs of life. Part of her wondered if something was lying in wait, ready to pounce on the unsuspecting traveler. Another part of her knew that nothing would live in such a cold and desolate place. It was an empty, forsaken location, and the further she traveled from the road, the lonelier she felt. She knew that was ridiculous because Jack was right next to her, but even he was unusually quiet.

"It's a long way from the village," she said. "Do you think they will deliver?"

"Deliver?"

"The takeaway."

Jack shook his head and she thought he meant no, but he was staring ahead as they turned a bend. In front of them stood an impressive looking house.

Stretching up three stories it seemed to reach for the heavens. On either side of the dark and imposing looking door were four windows on each floor. Moonlight reflected on the glass, turning the windows into mirrors that reflected the car back to them 32 times. It gave her the unsettling feeling that 32 hungry eyes all had them in their sights.

For a moment the house appeared rundown and overgrown, but it was as if a cloud passed over the moon and the place was back. Though old and worn, it was a beautiful and yet disturbing property that made her teeth feel as if they were vibrating like a tuning fork. The front door opened a crack and a couple appeared at the entrance. One seemed larger than the other, but at this distance, it was impossible to tell more. They stood on either side of the door as if on guard. For a moment she imagined that they were surrounded by malnourished children dressed in ragged clothes. Maybe she had spent too much time reading Rosie's notes as it seemed her mind was playing tricks on her.

"Where should I park?" Jack asked as the car trundled across the gravel toward them.

"I guess close to the door so we can unpack." Shelly wasn't sure. Right then she didn't want to be out in the open. It was just a feeling, as though something was watching them, waiting for the right moment. But the right moment for what?

Jack stopped the car as close as he could get. There was an overgrown garden between them and the front door, but it would do. He turned off the engine. The quiet was deafening.

"This is some place," he said. "Very remote. Are you sure about this?"

Shelly felt what he was feeling, she was sure of it. There was a pit in her stomach that was ice cold. The hairs on her arms were standing at attention, and there was a catch in her breath, pressure on her chest. Everything made her feel as if they should turn and go. But, she couldn't. She wouldn't. Not after all the time she had spent trying to find another spirit. Trying to prove that what she had seen was real and not just a figment of her imagination or a mirage brought on by grief and hope. She had to stay. Had to find out the truth and maybe, just maybe, one of these spirits could send a message for her. It was a slim hope, but it was all she had.

"I'm sure," she said as she opened the car door and grabbed her padded jacket. "Let's go meet the Duncans."

* * *

THERE WAS A NARROW, overgrown path leading up to the door of the house. As they left the car and stepped cautiously along it, cold seeped through their clothes and into their bones. It came with a heaviness that pressed down on her shoulders and made her want to turn and run. What was wrong with her? All this time she had hoped for a moment like this and now here she was, jumping at every shadow.

She was just tired. Excited and tired, but tired just the same. Maybe after a good night's sleep she would feel better.

Jack followed her along the path toward the door of the house.

At the door, the Duncans stood as still as statues. Their faces were hidden in shadow and it was hard to discern anything about them. The closer they got to the house the darker it became. It was as if the shadow of the place sucked away the moonlight, and that was when she noticed that there were no lights on inside the house. How strange was that?

She turned to tell Jack but he stumbled into her.

"Hurry up, it's cold out here," he said, and pushed her a little.

Shelly turned and rushed forward, shaking her leg as it snagged on a bramble.

The next few paces brought her face to face with the two elderly Duncans. As she had surmised, they were a man and a woman. Their skin was wrinkled and almost as white as their hair. It was impossible to tell how old they were but they looked ancient. They both wore black clothes consisting of long plain tops and matching trousers.

She smiled up at them. "Hi, I'm Shelly and this is Jack." She held out a hand but it waved in front of them, ignored. Slowly she let it fall. "Are you the Duncans?"

Eyes looming so dark that they were like pits of despair was the only answer she got. Silence fell between them and created a chasm.

Jack arrived at her side and coughed. He tried once again. "I'm Jack and this is Shelly. Is this RedRise House?"

"Yes." It was the man who answered but Shelly could have sworn his mouth never moved.

"We are expected. I emailed you," Shelly said.

"Yes, of course. The house has been waiting for you. Come on inside and we will show you around." The woman spoke and gave them a smile, but it never reached the pits of despair that were her eyes.

With a waft of her hand, she beckoned them into the house. The man turned and closed the door behind them. For a moment it was pitch black, and Shelly felt the cold hand of fear squeeze her heart so tightly that she thought it might burst.

Then a candle flared and shone upward, casting the old woman's face across the wall. Her mouth was distorted into a laugh, then a scream. Then she lit a lantern and the shadows disappeared.

Shelly shuffled on the spot... wondering what she should do... wondering if they should turn and run. As she had the thought she turned to the door. The man was standing there directly in front of it, blocking their escape with his dead black eyes and expressionless mouth.

"That's better," the woman said. "We keep having power cuts so you will need to use the gas lamps. Let me show you around."

Holding the lamp up, she showed them a large entrance hall. The floor was hardwood blocks polished to perfection.

The light flickered and chased crazy shadows across the walls. So much of the room was hidden that Shelly was sure that something was watching them. Sure that it lurked in the shadows, darting away as the lamp moved around the room.

Just as the lamp lit up the staircase the lights blinked and then came on. Shelly looked up to see a huge chandelier shining down at them and the room was suddenly beautiful.

With the light on, she raised her eyebrows at Jack, and he returned the gesture. They understood. Both had been a little panicked about what they would find but this... this was wonderful. Once more she was filled with confidence. There was nothing they couldn't handle.

"Ahh, that's better," the woman said, as she took off the glass from the lamp and extinguished the wick with her fingers. The smell of burning flesh wafted through the air and Shelly let out a gasp.

The woman pointed around the room. "This is RedRise House. It has been our home for many years... more than I can remember. Now it is empty, and some believe haunted."

"It is beautiful," Shelly said. "Isn't it, Jack?"

Jack nodded and clung onto the bag he was holding.

The hallways spread out before them as large as a ballroom. Across from them was a magnificent central staircase. It was carpeted in rich, deep burgundy and sentineled by two feet of dark wood, *mahogany,* she thought. The walls were a rich cream and large portraits hung all around. There were several of the man and woman, all looking very severe and austere. None of the portraits bore a smile. In some of the paintings there were lots and lots of children.

Were these the souls that were trapped here?

The woman walked toward the stairs. There was a heavy red rope on two brass plinths strung across the stairwell. It reminded Shelly of what they used at the nightclub to stop people from going in.

"Upstairs is off limits. The house is dangerous now, and you must not go up there."

Shelly jumped inside at the woman's voice, but she nodded.

Either side of the stairs was a passageway. Three doors led off to the left and two to the right.

"There is a bedroom, bathroom and sitting room down here which you may use." The woman pointed down the left corridor and then crossed to the right. "These rooms are off limits but the kitchen is here." She pointed to a door on the right-hand side of the entrance.

"It is fully stocked for you. Across from this room on the other side of the hall is the library. You may use it, but be very careful of the books. They are precious and irreplaceable. Do not damage them. Do you have any questions?"

Shelly could think of a hundred, but her mind wouldn't settle on just one.

Jack put down his case and turned toward the Duncans. It was not easy. They seemed to stay on both sides of them even though they didn't appear to be moving. Jack kept turning, trying to bring them both into view. It felt as if they were trying to stop them from leaving, and Shelly was filled with dread.

"What can you tell us about the history of the house?" Jack asked.

"You will find all you need to know in the library," the woman said and turned to walk away.

"We were hoping you could tell us your thoughts on the

house," Shelly said. "Have you seen any ghosts, any spirits? Or have you felt anything strange?"

"Of course," the woman said, and her voice was so cold it traced like ice down Shelly's spine.

"What have you seen?" Shelly asked, shaking away the cold as excitement gave her courage."

"You need to discover the house for yourselves," the man said.

Jack sighed and continued to move around in circles. Shelly was getting dizzy, but the Duncans didn't seem to move. Yet they could never see both of them at the same time.

"I understand that," she said turning to face the man. "I don't want you to give me any preconceived ideas, but a little history about the house will help."

"There is nothing we can tell you," the woman said, and Shelly jumped, turning around.

"Why not?" she asked.

"Because the house doesn't want you to be told," the man said, but Shelly was ready this time and she turned back slowly.

"I'm not asking the house. I'm asking you. Did children die here?"

"Not *here*," the man said, the smile that crossed his face gave her the heebie-jeebies.

He was hiding something, but even so, to hear him say that filled her with a mixture of disappointment and relief. The relief must be because who would want children to die in circumstances that would leave them in torment? But yet, it felt different.

"What about other deaths in the house?" Jack asked.

"Oh, people have died here, a lot of them." It was the woman this time, and they both turned like a never-ending carousel to look at her face.

Jack had gone white and his Adam's apple was bobbing as he gulped.

"What do you mean by that?" Shelly asked a little too harshly.

"It is a very old house." The carousel turned again.

"Can you tell us about the deaths?" Shelly asked the man and then turned back to the woman.

"People live. People die. The house goes on and on," she said. "Now, we must leave as we are old and tired and cannot keep going much longer. You have our email if you need anything." She handed Shelly a key and turned. With a nod to the man, they both walked to the door and through it, leaving it open.

Shelly smiled at Jack. "That was weird."

"They were super freaky." Jack walked to the door and held it open. "Where did they go?"

"What do you mean?" Shelly asked as she stepped out of the house. There was nothing there. Just the path leading to the driveway and their car parked at the end of it. The Duncans had simply vanished.

"Where did they go?" Jack asked again.

"They must have driven off."

Jack's eyebrows rose. "Really? I didn't see a car, did you?"

Shelly knew he was right. There had been no car. If they had walked then they would still be in sight. So where had they gone? That question filled her stomach with dread and she wondered if this was such a good idea after all.

CHAPTER 3

" $\mathcal{L}$ et's bring our gear in," Jack said as he walked back to the car.

Shelly nodded and followed him, but she had a real urge to tell him it had all been a mistake. That they should grab the bag from the house and just drive away. Maybe stop at a hotel somewhere and tell each other how they felt. But that was ridiculous. She was just having a batch of nerves and he would think she was crazy. All the effort she had put into getting here and now she didn't want to stay? This was insane. It was just a dark and empty house with a couple of creepy caretakers. Not one bit like some slasher horror movie. She laughed.

"What's funny?" Jack passed her a sleeping bag and a couple of pillows.

"Those two were pretty weird."

"I think they were hiding something, don't you?"

Shelly wondered about that. Maybe he was right and that's

all it was. "I bet they just need the money. They're likely trying to give the house an air of mystery, but really they're scared that we will leave and then this house will be just a drain once more."

"Did you have to pay them?"

Shelly cursed her own stupidity. She had been careful to keep that part of the arrangement to herself, but she should have known it would come out eventually. "Yes."

"How much?"

"Five hundred pounds." She held her breath waiting for him to shout at her. It was the money she had saved for next term's books. Without it, she would be in trouble. But her idea was that she could make that money back by selling their story, either to the press, or her favorite idea was to write a book and just sell the first few chapters to the press. "Don't be mad at me."

"I couldn't do that. And maybe you're right. They just tried to make it all mysterious but instead made it super creepy." He grabbed a couple more bags and nodded toward the door. "Or maybe they're hiding the dastardly deeds that have played out here. Hiding all the ghosts they know are here. Hiding the death in which this house is shrouded."

Shelly laughed. It was exactly what she had hoped to find, and yet the thought of it sent a chill down her back and left her stomach rolling as if in cold grease. Then she remembered that the old man had said: *no children had died here*. If that was right then how did Rosie see all the ghosts of children?

"They didn't even show us where our rooms are," Jack said, his arms still full of cushions and bags from the car.

31

Shelly hardly heard him. There was something about this place that didn't feel right. It didn't feel how she'd expected. What she wanted was excitement, a glimpse into another world with the chance to change things and to help others. What she felt was desolation and despair. Instead of exciting her it scared her, and that was something she had never come across before.

Jack put a hand on her shoulder.

Shelly jumped.

"Hey, I'm sorry. I didn't mean to scare you, but I have to admit this place gives me the willies."

Shelly nodded and tried to calm her racing heart. "I guess it should. It is a big ass haunted house, after all." She raised her eyebrows and mocked him a little. "The big bad ghost hunter scared of an empty house?"

Jack shrugged his shoulders. "Yes, a little." He winked, and it sent a different kind of shiver through her. "I guess I am a bit nervous but at least I've got you here to protect me."

He was mocking now and it lightened the mood. They both relaxed and felt more at ease.

"Why don't we get settled in and order some food," Jack said. "Now, where was our room again?"

"This way." Shelly grabbed a handful of gear and walked across the hardwood floor. Her footsteps echoed. The further she walked, the louder it got. The sound mocked her and conveyed to her how alone they really were. She wouldn't let this foolish weakness of hers destroy their chance to learn more. Finding out about ghosts, finding out how to communicate with them had been an obsession with her for years now. It was the most important thing in her life, and just a dark empty house wasn't gonna scare her away.

Behind her, she could hear Jack hurrying along, his footsteps shuffling across the floor. She could sense the fear he felt and was determined not to let it bother her, so she made her own steps confident. Tap, tap, tap, the sound of her heels echoed around the house and floated across the ether on and on and on, endlessly echoing.

Turning past the stairs the air felt colder, but she shrugged it off. It was a big house and there were bound to be drafts. The corridor leading away from them was lit by two small wall sconces. One was just at the start and the other halfway down the hallway. Beyond that was darkness. It gave the impression that the corridor went on forever. Ignoring the optical illusion, she walked along the hallway to the first door. It was on her right: a beautifully carved solid mahogany door. Turning the handle, she stepped inside. The room was pitch black. She had expected the light from the hallway to filter in and give her some view. Darkness surrounded her, as if the door had closed her in a tomb. Her breath caught in her throat, her heart pounded and for a moment she couldn't move. Dropping the gear, she turned and ran straight into Jack.

Jack let go of everything and grabbed hold of Shelly. "Hey, hey, you're okay," he whispered.

"It's so dark. I hate the dark." She really did. Things could hide in the dark... things that wanted to hurt you. She never knew where these thoughts came from... she had always been afraid of the dark, especially after what had happened before. But now she was acting stupid. She had to get a grip and control her emotions. After all, this was her dream. This was a job she had agreed to do and she was going to do it, no matter what the darkness held in store.

Light flooded the room and she was staring at Jack's smiling face. He raised his eyebrows and gave her a smile. "You are going to like this," he said.

Shelly nodded and stayed within the safety of his arms. Part of her wanted to stay there forever, but it was Jack who moved back and turned her around.

The room was magnificent. Romantic. Opulent. Sumptuous. "OMG, it's... it's amazing."

Before them was a huge room dominated by a four-poster bed. It was draped in the deepest crimson and finished with a heavy crimson comforter. Part of her wanted to squeal with delight. This was the sort of room that she had always dreamed of staying in and suddenly color touched her cheeks. This was the perfect room for a romantic getaway, just her and Jack, but that was not why they were here.

"This is amazing," she said again and turned around, being careful not to trip over their gear. Shelly was always tripping up, always getting lost, and always going places too quickly. But everything had brought her here. Suddenly the house felt right and all her fears were forgotten, for now.

As she turned she noticed the walls were a dark cream. The floor was mainly the same hardwood as the rest of the house, covered with a bright red shaggy rug. Blood red came to mind but she pushed the thought aside.

"There's only one bed," Jack said. "Did you mention... we're not a couple?"

Shelly wanted to shout, *why not*, but instead she shrugged. "I did. It doesn't matter. We've shared a room before. Sleeping bags." To push home the point, she picked one of the bags up and threw it onto the bed.

"Maybe that's another bedroom."

Shelly turned to see Jack was pointing at a door across the room on the left.

"Or that one." Jack pointed in the opposite direction.

Shelly hadn't noticed the doors when she turned around, but now they were as obvious as... doors.

"Let's explore." Stepping over their gear, she headed to the door on the right first. The handle was brass and cold to the touch. When she turned it there was resistance, and for a moment she imagined someone was holding the handle on the other side. Letting go, she gasped and stepped back.

"What's wrong?"

"It's cold. Made me jump," she said quickly.

"Here, let me." Jack stepped forward and turned the handle. "It's cold and stiff. Maybe it's swollen with the damp?"

He grunted and turned the handle and pushed the door open.

Once more the room was black inside, like a black hole that had sucked all the light from the universe and wouldn't let anymore enter. Why was she having such foolish thoughts? It was just a room with the light off.

Jack stepped in and fumbled in the darkness. She heard him pull a cord and a dull yellow light flickered for a few moments before brightening to the strength of a candle on a foggy day.

Shelly stepped into the somber looking room. It was small but lovely. The walls were half wood-paneled and painted in battleship gray. The floor was covered in gray quarry tiles. The main feature was a cast iron roll-top bath which stood on claw feet in the center of the room.

An antique sink stood below a round, cracked mirror next to the bath. The matching toilet stood on the other side of the bath. Then there were two matching white racks of white towels.

"Well, I'm looking forward to trying that out. It's huge," Jack said before turning and leaving the room.

Shelly found herself looking in the mirror. It showed a reflection of gray. Nothing but gray. And something about it disturbed her.

When Shelly turned, Jack was already at the other door. She wanted to shout, to warn him not to open it, but she couldn't. Her mouth opened but her throat was dry and no words came out. Why was she behaving like a school girl frightened of her own shadow?

Jack turned the handle and stepped into the other room. It was as if he had simply vanished. She raced across the bedroom to find him standing in a study. It was also a beautiful and luxurious room. She imagined sitting in it and looking over the notes and videos they would make. Feeling much better about things, she walked into the room and stared in awe.

It was an extravagant room with a large hardwood desk and an old-fashioned captain's chair. On the desk was a cream blotter in a leather frame and an antique ink pen rested on its own stand.

Looking around, she could see the walls were painted in a deep russet. It should have appeared dark and depressing.

Instead, it made the room look big and grand. The drapes were an even stronger orange-brown. They deeply complemented the walls. Ignoring the urge to run her fingers over the curtains, she took in the four chairs upholstered in velvet that matched the curtains, they were arranged around the room. On the hardwood floor there was a pale ochre shag pile rug that she had the sudden urge to stand on in her bare feet and wiggle her toes. It would no doubt feel wonderful.

"No bed, so it looks like we're sharing," she said and turned to see Jack flush crimson. Ignoring him, she went back into the bedroom and started sorting out their gear. "Let's put this lot away and then we can order some food. While we're waiting we can set up the cameras."

"Sounds like a plan," Jack said from behind her.

Quickly she arranged her sleeping bag on the right side of the bed. She always slept on that side. She knew she had her quirks and this was one of them. She had to sleep on her left side and liked to sleep closest to the edge of the bed and, if possible, facing the door. So, she chose the side with two doors hoping that Jack would guard the other one for her.

Grabbing her pillows, she placed them on the bed only to find that Jack was laying his sleeping bag down on the floor.

"What are you doing?" she asked.

A blush chased across his cheeks, and he lowered his head and cleared his throat. These were all signs of discomfort and she hated to see him like this.

"Jack, we shared a bed all through the trial with no difficulties. There is a separate bathroom, so what is the problem?"

He cleared his throat again and looked up at her. "I think it's better if I stay down here. The bed... well that bed..."

Shelly understood what he meant. The bed was designed for romance. Still, she was annoyed.

An uneasy silence grew between them as they packed away their gear. Once it was done they stood facing each other, the silence growing.

This was ridiculous. Shelly pulled out her phone. "What are we eating?"

Jack laughed, relieved. They were back on easy ground. "I could manage with just a foo yung, but knowing how hungry you always are... should we share a set meal for three?"

Shelly nodded and clicked the stored number.

"I just don't know where you put it. You're like a bottomless pit."

"Thanks," she said, wishing he would think of her in other terms, but before she could say anything the restaurant answered.

Shelly ordered the meal. "What's the address for delivery?" the young girl asked.

"RedRise House, it's..."

"We know where it is. I'm not sure the driver will go out there."

Now what? Shelly thought. "Is it too far?"

"No..."

Silence mocked her. "Hello, are you still there?"

"Yes... the house has a reputation. Most of the locals are afraid of it. You shouldn't be there."

"Oh, don't worry. We're professional ghost hunters. We know what we're doing." Even though she sounded confident, Shelly was disturbed by the warning. But why? She knew this house was haunted. That was their whole reason for coming here.

"Let me check with the driver. He's just come in."

Shelly heard her put the phone down and raised her eyebrows at Jack. He was standing there looking like a lost puppy. Maybe he had realized how insulting his bottomless pit and stick insect analogies were, but he couldn't say anything yet to make her feel better.

"Hello. Yes, the driver says he will deliver, but it will be an extra fiver. Is that okay?"

Shelly thought about it; they could probably drive and collect the meal cheaper, but if she left the house would she dare come back in? "That's fine."

"Great. It will be about an hour."

"Thanks." The phone had already gone dead, so she popped her own phone back in her pocket and turned to Jack. "About an hour."

"Lovely. I... I... look I didn't mean you were like a bottomless pit or a stick insect as I said earlier. You are beautiful and a real woman... I just meant... well I wanted to say..."

"I know what you meant and I'm just torturing you. I've always needed to eat loads to keep at this weight. Most of the time it's great, but occasionally I just wish I could eat a little less. It would be a bit easier on the food budget."

"I never thought I'd hear someone say that," Jack laughed.

Shelly nodded and laughed with him. The awkwardness had gone. "Let's set up the laptop in the office and then some cameras around the house."

Jack nodded and followed her into the office. Shelly moved the blotter, but as she did it caught the light and she saw the indentations of what had previously been written on it. For a moment she was intrigued. "Look!"

Jack took it from her. "I see. Do you have a pencil? We can do a rubbing." He placed the blotter down and made the motions with his hand.

Shelly wanted to laugh but she knew he would be upset. He could be so sensitive at times. It was one of the things she loved about him. So, she turned quickly, grabbed her bag and pulled out a pencil.

Jack lightly rubbed the pencil across the paper and let out a gasp. He dropped the pencil and stepped back.

Shelly peered over his shoulder and felt her blood turn to ice.

CHAPTER 4

*H*er eyes narrowed, and the words swam in and out of focus. Surely she couldn't be seeing this, surely it was a mistake. "J... Jack is that what you see?"

"I see it," he said. "Though I wish I didn't."

Showing white against the gray of the pencil was Die, Die, Die, Die, Die, Die, Die, Die, Die, Die, Die, Die, Die, Die, Die, Die, Die, Die, Die, Die, Die, Die, Die, Die, Die, Die, Die, Die, Die, Die, Die, Die, Die, Die, Die. Over and over again.

Shelly picked up the pencil and traced more lead across the rest of the page. Sure enough, the words continued. Some were small, some large, some in capitals but all down the page was just that one word.

Die, Die, Die, DIE, Die, Die, Die, Die, Die, Die, Die, DIE, DIE, DIE, DIE, Die, Die, Die, Die, die, Die, Die, die, DIE, Die, Die, die, Die, Die, Die, die, Die, Die, Die, Die, Die, DIE.

Then it dawned on her. "This has to be the Duncan's they

have done this to scare us. At least they didn't write all work and no play makes Jack a dull boy."

Shelly was laughing now, she had almost convinced herself that was the truth.

Jack looked less convinced.

"We could always leave."

"No way, miss out on all that lovely Chinese."

Jack shrugged. "It was just a thought, so you really think it was that creepy old couple? That they would have enough of a sense of humor to do this?"

"Not the sense of humor, they probably don't even see the significance, they have probably never watched The Shining, but they did this."

"What if they didn't?"

Shelly's heart missed a beat, but she laughed. "Isn't that why we're here?"

Jack nodded.

Shelly grabbed the cameras and recording equipment they had. It wasn't much. She had borrowed a bit from the university, without asking, and had an old camcorder. Then she had got some webcams that she was going to set up wirelessly. She reckoned she could cover the hallway, maybe some of the upstairs rooms, the kitchen and one or two in here. All she had to decide was where to start.

The problem was they hadn't covered anything like this in her course, and she was lost. Dithering on the spot, she started to wonder if Jack was right. *No, fear was stupid.*

"So, where do we start?" Jack asked.

"We will set a couple up in these rooms and then find the kitchen."

"Nice to see you have your priorities sorted."

Shelly nodded and soon they had one camera set up to cover the office and entrance to the bedroom. The other one covered some of the bedroom and some of the bathroom. She checked they were linked to the laptop and then set off back down the hall.

"Slow down," Jack called as he hurried after her.

Shelly peered over her shoulder and laughed but kept going. If she slowed down the incessant tap, tap, tap of her footsteps would drive her insane.

Crossing the entrance hall, it got even worse. The tap, tap seemed to surround her. It was as if an army of footsteps were converging on her location. Ignoring the hallway opposite them, she crossed to the door which had to be the kitchen.

Opening the door, she scrabbled for a light switch. The wall felt cold, damp and she wanted to pull her hand away but she couldn't, just as panic was taking over, she found the switch and clicked it on.

The light revealed a large kitchen. There were red slates on the floor. A huge range cooker and deep mahogany units. The sink was old fashioned and ceramic the steel taps looked antique.

Looking around she saw a kitchen table and chairs an old dresser and behind them two doors. One was in the corner of the room and the other the middle of the same wall. She went to the left one first and for a moment didn't want to open it.

Then Jack was behind her. "That will be the pantry, my gran has a kitchen just like this. He opened the door to a small room packed with shelves full of tins and other items.

"I hope you feel like cooking," she said.

Jack laughed. "I know you won't. You never stand still long enough to cook a meal."

"I like things burned," she said and gave him a smile. "What's behind door number two?"

They both walked over to the door in the corner. There was a note pinned to it.

This room is out of bounds.
Do not enter.

"What the...?"

"Shelly," Jack admonished. "I imagine it's the cellar and it's probably unsafe. We should stay out of it."

"Really!?"

Jack knew her well enough, to know that wasn't happening, but before she could say anything, there was a knock at the door.

"Food at last," she said and raced for the door.

Shelly opened the big heavy door to find nothing but black, the expected delivery driver was nowhere to be seen. Peering out, she could hardly see the tangled front garden. Light from the inside stopped at the threshold.

Hunger growled in her stomach, and she sighed with frustration. *Where was he?* She peered out as far as she could without stepping from the light. It was no use. If the guy had wandered around trying to find them, then he wouldn't see her.

"Hello," she called, her voice weak and ineffectual.

Pulling her phone from her pocket, she stepped out and shut the door. Using the phone as a torch, she wandered back to the gravel where Jack's car was parked. There she hoped to see another car. There was nothing, the drive was bare except for the Clio. So who had knocked?

* * *

JACK WATCHED SHELLY RUN from the kitchen like a kid chasing Christmas. She was so excited over a simple takeaway. He took a few moments and crossed to the cupboards. Opening a few doors, he soon found plates and cutlery. He set these on the table and was about to see where Shelly was when there was another knock at the door.

"Shel, did you get that?" he called, but there was no answer. The silence in the house was driving him mad. He would have to get out a portable speaker and set up some music. Anything would be better than this emptiness. Especially when he felt so inadequate around her. How he wanted to tell her that they should try and be more than friends, that he wanted more, but it never seemed to be the right time. Maybe at the end of this stay, he would pluck up the courage.

There was another knock at the door. He crossed the vast hall wondering if she had locked herself out by mistake. "On my way."

He opened the door with a big smile on his face, it wasn't Shelly who stood there, but a priest.

"Oh," he said and stepped back. Heat flooded his cheeks, and he grinned an apology. "Sorry I was expecting someone else. Can I help you?"

The man gave a friendly smile. "I understand, it is dark and lonely here. I just wanted to see what you were doing, why you were here? My name is Nick Aubrey. I'm the local priest."

Jack stepped back a little. The man looked in his early thirties. He had short dark hair and a friendly smile. An old-fashioned black suit hung loosely on his lean frame, and his dog collar shone like a beacon in the darkness.

What was a priest doing here and why was he asking such questions?

"I'm here with my girlfriend... well she's a girl and my friend if you know what I mean. Why are you asking?"

The priest gave him a placating smile and shook his head. There was something about the way he wouldn't hold eye contact, and he constantly looked behind him.

"Is Shelly alright?" Jack asked as fear flared in his gut.

"I don't know a Shelly, I need to talk to you especially if you have a girl here. Would you please step outside and give me a few minutes of your time?"

"Girl... Shelly is a woman really, not a girl." Jack knew he was making a mess of things. He was confident when it came to anything but Shelly. Around her, talking about her, he was like the village idiot. It was as if his brain melted just at the thought of her.

"I understand." The priest stepped back. "If you would just step outside and give me a few minutes of your time."

"No, if you want to talk you can come into the kitchen." Jack opened the door a little wider and stepped to one side.

The man looked uncomfortable. He glanced behind Jack and looked at the house as if he was afraid. For a moment Jack thought that he would turn and run but in the end, he nodded his head and stepped across the threshold.

Jack shut the door behind him. "Shelly we have company," he called but the words fell on an empty house... he was sure. Where had she gone, to the car for something?

"If you follow me we can sit in the kitchen." Jack led the way into the kitchen and pointed Nick to a seat. "Can I get you a drink?" he asked out of politeness.

"No, no thank you. I wouldn't eat or drink anything from such an accursed place."

"Okay," Jack said, "I think you should leave."

"Please, hear me out, but where is your friend? I would like her to hear this too."

Jack nodded despite himself. Whatever this man had to say he suddenly wanted Shelly to hear it too. "Let me check the bedroom, maybe she's there."

The priest nodded, Jack left the room. He was starting to worry about Shelly. She was never quiet, never far away and she moved about so quickly that if she had gone to check on the equipment, she would be back. Had she gone outside when the knock came earlier?

Jack knocked on the bedroom door and entered when there was no answer. The room was empty. The bathroom was also empty. He moved across the rug and peered into the office it was also empty. *Where was she?*

Panic spiked inside, he rushed back to the hallway and into the kitchen. Fear and panic were like twin horses racing through the night and pulling a cartload of dread. Had this man done something to her? He turns up, and Shelly goes missing, it had to be more than a coincidence.

"Is something wrong," Nick asked.

"My friend, did you do something to her?"

"Jack."

Jack turned to see Shelly standing in the door of the kitchen. Her hands were shaking, her skin was white as paper. "Where have you been?" he said too harshly, and she backed away.

The priest stood and took her hands. "Come sit for a moment, and then we will get you out of here, both of you."

* * *

SHELLY COULDN'T FIND ANYONE, and it took her a while to make it back to the house. It was so dark, so very dark that even the phone's torch app could hardly chase away the blackness.

Once inside she could hear voices. She followed them to the kitchen. Jack was upset. She could see it in the set of his shoulders and the way he clenched his jaw but who was the man sat next to him?

"Jack," she managed.

Jack turned. "Where have you been?" he barked at her the anger even more apparent. Without realizing it, she moved back.

Someone took her hands, and she blinked to see a strange man stood in front of her.

"Come sit for a moment, and then we will get you out of here, both of you."

"What do you mean get out of here?" she said as she pulled her hands from his.

"My name is Nick Aubrey. I have been the priest for this district for... for a long while. You need to leave and now, while you can."

Shelly winked at Jack and pulled out a chair across from the priest. She sat down and pointed for him to do the same. He sat, and so did Jack.

"Shelly leaned forward. Jack and I are ghost hunters we are exactly where we want to be. We are here to research this house and to put the spirits here to rest. If you can help in that matter by providing us with some history, then please tell us all you know."

"Do you not see the danger you are in," Nick said. "Do you not see that many have died in this house and that if you don't leave you will not free the spirits... you will join them?"

Shelly could swear the air was sucked from the room as he said the words. It was hard to breathe. It felt as if her lungs were being crushed. She would not let him know that he rattled her. "I see that you want to scare us. I would ask that you help us rather than simply try and chase us away."

The lights dimmed, and the house was plunged into darkness.

Shelly let out a squeal and the room filled with evil. The presence was like mist in the darkness. There but unseen.

You could feel it. Could almost reach out and touch it but still, there was only the deepest blackness she had ever seen.

Light filled the room, and she could see that Jack had pulled his phone from his pocket and activated the torch app.

Nick Aubrey's face was a mask of fear. He believed what he was saying, and so did she. Part of her wanted to run, to do as he said, but this was her big chance and this only made her more interested.

Torchlight lit up the table but the darkness pressed against the beam.

"I have to go," Nick said, his chair scraped across the floor as he stood.

Bit by bit the dark encroached onto the light. Nick stepped closer to the table, to stay inside the light.

Shelly wanted to run, but she feared that dark touching her. She tried to reach for her own phone, but her hand was shaking so badly she couldn't hold it. Should they run or should they stay and face this?

The lights came on, the house was once more normal.

"Do you see what I mean?" Nick asked as he stood there shaking.

"It's just the power going out," Shelly said with a laugh. "The Duncan's warned us about it. Now, why don't you tell us a bit about the house, to help us with our job?"

"Please leave with me now."

Jack shook his head. "No, we can't do that. Why not help us out?"

"There is a book, The Sacrifices of RedRise House and the

Rise of Old Hag, it tells the story of the house by those of us who were here. Even I have written in its pages, but please leave this place before it is too late."

"We cannot do that," Shelly said. "The book is not here. It is in an evidence locker in Leeds. However, we have heard much of what is in this book but to hear it from someone else would be very useful. Each person has their own take on a subject. Please tell us your tale, please help us."

"I cannot help you if you are too foolish to see. I will stay close, but please leave before it is too late."

"There's no need to be rude." Shelly couldn't believe the man. What right did he have to call them fools? Her eyes flicked to Jack, she could see he was angry. Once more color had risen on his cheeks, and there was tension in his jaw.

"She's right there was no need for that. I want you to leave." Jack stood and crossed his arms.

"I'm sorry." Nick shook his head. "I will not stay here a moment longer. Just promise me one thing. When things start to happen get out of here quickly. You will find my residence via a path behind the house. Find me if you need me but don't risk your lives."

"We can handle this," Shelly said, but she wondered why he was so afraid.

Nick nodded before quickly walking to the door.

Then he was gone.

Shelly and Jack sat alone in the silence.

CHAPTER 5

"*D*o you think we should leave?" Jack asked as the silence was once more deafening.

Shelly shook her head, but she was wondering the very thing herself. Maybe they could stay somewhere local and just come back during the day. The house was super creepy when the power went out. Then again, was she just being paranoid, allowing her fear of the dark to rule her? There was nothing else to be afraid of. The Old Hag, the spirit who had once terrorized this house and held children here, was gone. The children she killed and kept here wanted their help. They needed their help, they should stay. Before she could say any of that, there was another knock at the door.

They both jumped and then laughed.

"Takeaway?" Jack said.

"God I hope so, I couldn't cope with anything else tonight."

They crossed to the door to see a slim man about their age.

His eyes were flicking behind him, and he kept turning his head.

"How much? Jack asked.

"£27.50."

Jack gave him a twenty and ten and took the bag. "Keep the change." It was warm and smelt delicious.

The man snatched the money and scuttled down the path to disappear into the darkness.

"Thank you," Jack called after his scurrying back.

"Maybe he's late," Shelly said as she took the food back to the kitchen.

She stopped as she entered. "Where did that come from?" She pointed at one of the kitchen chairs.

Curled up there was a black cat. Shelly left the food with Jack and ran over scooping it up into her arms. "Hey there," she whispered as the cat purred in reply and rubbed against her cheek.

"Oh, you are cold." She cuddled him close while Jack served up the food.

The smell of beef and mushrooms in black bean sauce wafted through the kitchen and all their fears were chased away on countless good memories.

Jack placed two plates on the table, his had just the beef in black bean, a little foo yung, and a few chips. Shelly's plate had the beef, foo yung, sweet and sour chicken, ribs, rice and a large portion of chips.

"Will that be enough for you," he said with a chuckle.

"Just about right." She started tucking into the food by eating her chips with one hand and still cuddling the cat with her other. Jack grabbed two glasses of wine before he sat down.

"To our first ghost hunt," he said raising a glass.

"Our first ghost hunt." Shelly took a big swig of the wine and closed her eyes. "This is wonderful."

As they ate, they discussed what they would do tomorrow or even later that night.

"I want to review the exorcisms from the book we brought," Shelly said.

"That sounds like a good idea... do you think we'll need them?" Jack had turned white again.

"I imagine so... if any spirits show."

"Here's hoping." He raised his glass of wine. "Our first ghost hunt."

"Our first ghost hunt." They clinked glasses.

"We should get out the Ouija board and do a séance," Shelly said.

"Do you think that's a good idea?" Jack downed the wine in his glass and left the table to grab the bottle.

"I do. So far we have had no spirit activity, and that is why we're here."

Jack topped up both of their glasses. "What about the priest, about his warning?"

Shelly took a sip and rolled it in her mouth while she thought. "I'm not even sure he is a priest. Did he look weird to you?"

I guess... he looked old fashioned, but it's hard to tell now. Maybe it's because he's from the country and doesn't get out much."

"Maybe. There was just something... I couldn't put my finger on it, but some of the things he said didn't ring true."

Jack nodded. "I know what you mean. Maybe his church doesn't approve. Maybe they heard we were coming and they want to stop us."

Shelly got up the cat was meowing in her arms. "Do you think he's hungry?"

"Maybe, maybe he's lost and snuck in and got caught."

Shelly found a few pieces of chicken and scraped them into one of the trays. As she put it on the floor, the cat leaped from her arms and straight to the dish.

Shelly watched him for a moment. Then she cleared the plates from the table before sitting down. It gave her time to think and at last, it came to her. The thing he had said that just couldn't be true.

"Remember what Rosie told us about that book, *The Sacrifices of RedRise House and The Rise of Old Hag?*"

"Not all of it." Jack shrugged.

"She said the last entry was made over a hundred years ago and here is this so-called priest telling us he wrote in it. I think we caught him out."

Jack laughed. "Unless of course, he's another ghost."

Shelly laughed as well. "That would be funny. What should we do now?"

Jack shrugged again. "I don't know, what should we do?"

"We have to wait, and you know how good I am at that."

Jack rolled his eyes and then winked. It made Shelly's knees go weak, she was glad she was sat down. Jack was so good to her. He knew how impatient she was. How she hated waiting for anything and yet that was all they could do now. Sit and wait for the spirits to make contact unless they helped with that. "Should we get out the Ouija board?"

Jack put down his glass of wine, the smile fell off his face.

Was he scared?

"I'm a touch tired tonight. I bought a Blu-ray of paranormal activity. We could curl up on the bed and watch it on the laptop." He picked up the half-empty bottle of wine. "And we could finish this. Start in earnest tomorrow when we're a bit more rested."

"That sounds like a fab idea." Shelly got up and looked for the cat. "Where'd he go?"

They both looked around, but the cat was nowhere to be found.

Shelly followed Jack back to the room. She was pleased that he had suggested such a romantic interlude. She was also pleased to be going back to the bedroom. It was like a little oasis, they could shut out the creepy house and the weird people and forget ghosts for just one night. As she had the thought she was filled with a mix of emotions. Disappointment at herself for giving in but also fear of what lay ahead and relief at not dealing with it for tonight. She was such a worry-wart. Never happy.

Soon they lay on the bed, sipping wine and watching the movie. They were so close but not quite touching. Still, she could feel her breath coming too fast and was sure he would hear the sound of her pounding heart. This was turning out to be a wonderful excursion, and this was just the first night.

The camera shook, and something darted across the screen. Shelly let out a squeal and grabbed Jack's arm. He jumped as well and then they were both laughing as the laptop bounced off his legs.

"Sorry, but I love this film," Shelly said.

Jack raised his left arm and nodded his head for her to lean against him. Shelly snuggled into his shoulder and said nothing as he reached down and pulled the laptop back. Her heart was pounding overtime now. Some of it was for the scene she knew was coming, but most of it was the feel of his shoulder beneath her head and the touch of his arm around her. Jack would protect her from anything.

Shelly tensed as she waited for Toby to creep toward the bed. It was such a scary scene and one that had given her nightmares for weeks after she first saw it. Now here she was in a haunted house and watching it again. What was wrong with her?

She held her breath as the shadow crept across the screen. On the bed, the unsuspecting person slept. Shelly leaned forward wanting to shout at Alex to wake up, wanting to shake her. Just as the spirit appeared the sound of piano keys came from within the house.

"Did you hear that?" Shelly asked. She could see from the look on Jack's face that he had.

"Was it on the film?" he asked.

"No, I've seen it a few times, that was not on it."

Jack paused the film. They listened for long seconds there

was nothing, they both started to smile. Then it came again a discordant jumble of notes that raised the hair on her arms and filled her stomach with ice.

"What was that?"

"A piano?"

"I don't think there's one in the house. Rosie would have said."

Jack eased forward straining to hear. "Maybe she didn't have time to tell us everything, maybe it's upstairs."

"Yes, but the house is empty."

CHAPTER 6

"What should we do?" Shelly asked and then regretted the words. This was why she was here, why they were both here. To investigate the unknown and the unexplainable. To find the spirits of the children and to set them free and here she was jumping like a child on a ghost train.

"Remember what Nick said, maybe we should grab our things and go." Jack had closed the laptop and was reaching for his jacket.

"No, we need to go see what it is. Maybe it's the children trying to send us a signal. To let us know they are here."

Jack's Adam's apple bounced as he swallowed. "Couldn't they do it in the daylight?"

Shelly shook her head and laughed. She knew what to do, and she was feeling better already. Pulling her mobile out of her pocket she turned on the camera. They would record what happened, and they would have their proof. "Come on this is what we wanted."

The corridor was dark and yet she could have sworn they left the light on. Ignoring the feelings of dread, she headed for the stairs with nothing but the light of her phone. The noise had definitely come from upstairs. It was somewhere just above them so they would have to turn left at the top. She turned to see that Jack was following.

He had grabbed a torch and a bottle of Holy Water and was fumbling with them as he hurried along. Almost juggling and it brought a smile to her lips. They were a great team. He had remembered the equipment, where she was all courage and rushing into danger.

The torch came on behind her throwing her shadow forward, it reared up like a gargoyle and set her heart racing. It was just a shadow, and yet at the thought of danger, it turned into something more. She slowed down, and Jack almost bumped into her as she stopped at the bottom of stairs.

They were dark and stretched up before them. Feeling along the wall, she flicked on three light switches. Nothing happened for long moments, she wondered if the power had gone again. Then gradually the chandelier came to life. It was as if it was powered by gas and took a while to come to full pressure. Slowly the light got bright enough to chase away the shadows. Then the hall lights followed sluggishly coming to power, and lastly, the lights on the stairs lit up one at a time. Gradually revealing more and more of the staircase and eventually the landing above. It looked so empty, so desolate and she wanted to turn and run.

"Have you heard anything else?" Jack asked.

Shelly jumped and let out a little shriek.

"Sorry." He smiled and shrugged.

Shelly let out a breath. "The atmosphere is getting to me. We should be quiet, we don't want to scare anything away."

Jack nodded and moved forward to unhook the rope that prevented them from ascending the stairs.

He nodded again and indicated for Shelly to go first only she couldn't move. Her knees had frozen in place, and she couldn't breathe. What if something was up there? What did she really think she could do? She glanced at the door of the house, and for a moment she wanted to run, then remembered a night six years ago.

The terrible storm, the desolation, and then the sound of her sister's voice. Telling her to try harder. To get up and move. It had been a miracle, had changed everything and had given her this drive to help spirits. Shaking her head, she cleared the memory. This was not the time to be looking back. It was time to go up those stairs and to help those children find peace.

Smiling at Jack, she pressed record on the phone and started to walk up the stairs. They were brightly lit and yet the higher she climbed, the darker it seemed. Her feet sank into the plush carpet on the first few steps. The wood of the stairs shone with polish but as she climbed the carpet became thin and threadbare. Her feet could hardly feel it and what they did feel was slick and loose in places. The wood on the stairs was cracked and peeling. Ignoring the feeling of despair that threatened to crush her she kept walking. This was what she wanted, what she had worked for and she would not give in to her fear.

As she neared the top of the stairs, the piano tinkled again, and she stopped dead. Jack almost rushed into the back of her. She could feel the heat from his breath on her neck, and it gave her courage.

Letting out a breath of her own she noticed the air mist before her. When had it got so cold? Then she understood, it meant there was a spirit close.

"Look at our breath," she said and moved the phone, so it recorded the mist they were both making.

Jack's jaw was set tight. She could see the fear in his eyes, but he nodded, supporting her and she turned the camera back and took another step on the slimy carpet. She was both terrified and excited. Wanting to run forward and run away at the same time.

"Just promise me one thing. When things start to happen, get out of here quickly," the priest's voice was clear in her mind. She wanted to do as he bid, but she couldn't do that. She couldn't let Stacey down.

Holding her breath and ignoring the urge to rub her arms she took another step.

The sound of a child crying echoed from above, she almost stopped, but she knew if she did that would be it. She would run from this house and never return. Slowly she kept moving, hoping that the phone would record the sound.

Her breathing was ragged now, would drown out the crying. As she took another step, a shadow darted across the top of the staircase.

"Did you see that?" she whispered and felt Jack's arm on her shoulder. His fingers were warm, clammy even.

"We should leave," he whispered in return. "We can come back in daylight."

"No." Shelly had said the word before she could think and now she regretted it. She wanted to leave, was afraid to stay but how could she leave when this was what she wanted. She took another step and wondered if she should call out to the children. It seemed like a good idea.

"We are here to help you, to free you. Show yourself."

The words echoed above her, she took another step. The stairs creaked, and a single D flat sounded in the silence. It hung in the air mocking her.

Taking another step she listened. The note faded and nothing else could be heard. Not even creaking or the wind outside. There was no sound of traffic, they were too remote for that, but she didn't think she had ever heard just nothing.

She took another step and another. There were only three steps to go now, she could hardly draw breath. Her chest was tight, her heart pounded so hard against her ribs she wondered if it would burst. If she didn't move now, then she would turn and run. So she took the next three steps in quick succession and turned left. There was another staircase leading up into darkness and a long empty corridor with doors leading off on both sides. She looked around. Jack was just behind her and behind that was an identical corridor. For a moment she imagined a creepy kid pedaling a scooter along it. *Stop it.* She had to shake the vision from her head.

"What now?" Jack asked, Shelly almost screamed.

Taking a deep breath, she got ahold of herself before she replied. "We check the rooms and see if we can find a piano."

They started along the corridor.

The sound of laughter echoed through the night. It was not a nice sound but mocking, cruel, and it turned her stomach to ice and her knees to jelly.

Ignoring the laughter, she walked on, the phone held out in front of her. The picture through the phone looked so different. So stark and eerie that she had to look away from it.

They came to the first door, it was open. Inside was an old piano. The lid was up and as they watched one of the keys depressed, and a sad note echoed around the room.

"Let me help you," she said.

The piano lid slammed shut, and the door slammed shut in front of them. From below them came the sound of a scream and a crash.

"What was that?" Jack asked.

"It came from our room."

"We have to leave," he said and grabbed her hand.

Shelly let him pull her back toward the stairs, but somehow she knew that they would not be able to leave. She had been a fool and had made a terrible mistake, and she wondered if she would live long enough to tell him she was sorry.

CHAPTER 7

*J*ack pushed Shelly in front of him and looked behind them. Why had he let her persuade him to stay? Why had he let her persuade him to come here?

The corridor was darker now. The lights fading and he turned and raced after her.

Shelly reached the top of the stairs and turned to run down them. The sight of her, just feet ahead of him, filled him with love as her ponytail swung behind her. Fast on her feet and so brave she shamed him with his gut full of fear and shaking legs. She disappeared from his view, and the darkness caught him.

Panic weakened his legs, but he pushed on as fast as he could and yet the further he ran the further he had to go. Pumping his arms, he pushed faster, harder. A shadow appeared in front of him, just a hole in the darkness, but before he could stop it was gone. Something touched his ankle and then he was falling.

The torch spun out of his hands, spiraling in the air like a crazy disco light, it landed on the thin carpet with a clank. Wheeling his arms, desperate to stay upright he plummeted after it, but it was no use. He was going down and hit the carpet hard enough to slam his shoulder into the floor and to knock the air from his lungs. The bottle of Holy Water was still clutched in his fingers, and his first thought was about the glass and injury.

It was fine, still intact.

Gasping for breath, he tried to stand to follow Shelly but something grabbed his ankle. Then he remembered the feel of something on his leg just before he fell. Someone, something had tripped him, and now it wanted him.

"No." Kicking out he tried to push it away. The pressure released off his ankle and he scrambled toward the stairs. It wasn't far, and yet it seemed further than they had walked to the room and he had been running for how long? It seemed like forever. This made no sense.

"Shelly, get out of here," he shouted, but the words were swallowed by the darkness.

Torch, where was his torch? It had landed just in front of him. Turning he spotted the oasis of light and scrambled toward it. The carpet was slimy beneath his knees and hands. Part of him imagined it as wet skin, and he wanted to get away from it and take a long hot shower, but that was after he got out of this God-forsaken hellhole.

On and on he crawled, the carpet so thin he could feel the wood beneath it, but he was getting closer. The torch had landed with the beam pointing away from him. It made little dint in the cold, black, hell he had found himself in. But he crawled faster, it was weak, but it was hope and so close.

A shadow crossed in front of the torch but before he could react something cold grabbed his ankle. This time the grip was strong and no matter how he kicked he couldn't free his leg. Still, he tried, kicking and grunting he lashed out at the darkness, but there was nothing there. No matter how hard he kicked, his legs contacted with nothing but the floor and yet the pressure on his ankle was still there.

It was like bony fingers squeezing so hard they would surely break the bone. The fingers jerked him, and he was flipped onto his back. Raising his arms, he held the Holy Water out in front of him expecting an attack, but nothing came. Nothing was there just the terrible darkness that hid everything.

Once more he was jerked and then dragged away from the stairs. Panic flared inside, but there was no time. The carpet burned against his back and his head smashed into the floor stunning him for a moment.

"Help me, Jesus help me," he screamed into the night as he was dragged along the floor away from the torches beam and into the darkness.

Was this the end?

* * *

JACK PUSHED SHELLY PAST HIM, she didn't hesitate. Something was happening, and she knew she had to record it. Fear and excitement raced inside her, so far they were neck and neck. There was also a touch of anger. She was here to help these children, but they were messing with her. The carpet slipped beneath her feet, and for a moment she was falling. Fear raced ahead, and she let out a yelp, but she landed on her right leg, though it gave slightly, she stayed on her feet.

The extra momentum swept her down the last few steps, she landed hard on the wooden floor. Without hesitating, she ran down the corridor and burst into their room. The laptop was on the floor. The screen flashing and anger was back in the lead but only for moments. As she approached the laptop, she saw six pairs of bare and dirty feet.

A hand squeezed her lungs, expelling all the air. Gasping she stared at the feet but was aware that the room was filled with a high pitched keening sound. It grated on her nerves. She looked up. There were three girls and three boys, standing girl, boy, girl, boy, girl boy. The girls wore dark, old-fashioned work dresses. The aprons that hung over them were tattered and stained. The boys had dark trousers, patched at the knees, that didn't quite reach their skinny ankles, and they wore some form of smock top. As she looked at them, the fear changed to pity. They were wretchedly thin and looked so frightened with their heads bowed and their dirty, matted hair.

"I'm here to help you," she whispered but doubted they could hear it above the keening noise.

Where was it coming from? What was making it?

Shelly realized that she still held the phone, but it was pointed down at the ground. Lifting it, she looked at the children through it. At either side of them was a tall shadowy figure that stopped her breath in her throat.

Shelly looked back at the children, the shadows had gone. Back through the phone and they were there. Difficult to see, they moved, coalesced and shifted, but something was holding the children here. They were pinned between darkness — she had to save them.

How she hoped that this was being recorded for it was exactly what she needed to prove Rosie's innocence.

"How can I help you?" she asked.

The keening stopped, and the children all raised their heads.

Shelly began to scream as she saw the deep slashes at each of their throats. Blood ran from some of the wounds, others were simply dirty, crusty holes that began to flap as the keening started once more.

It is your turn, a voice said inside her head. You help us by joining us.

Shelly ran from the room and only then did she realize that Jack was missing. The children had separated them, and now she was to be sacrificed. Was Jack already dead?

CHAPTER 8

"*I* wish you could have been there," Gail said as she reached across the table and took Rosie's hand. "I know we haven't known each other long, but we have become such good friends."

Rosie put her other hand on top of Gail's and squeezed. "Thank you, but it's all right. I know you all feel sorry for me, don't, I'm free. Living with Matron inside of me was a much worse prison than this. Now show me the ring." Rosie pulled her hands away.

Gail laughed and lifted her left hand off the oak table to better show off her ring. She loved it so much, had loved it before she saw it but when she did, she was blown away. Jesse knew her so well, the ring was everything she wanted. Pretty and yet practical. Six diamonds surrounded a rose ruby and were all set in rose gold which made even the diamonds glow with warmth.

"I love it so much," Gail said. "Almost as much as I love this chappy here."

"Oh stop it," Jesse closed his grey eyes and turned an unmanly shade of pink. With his brown hair shorn so short, you could see that even his head was blushing. "Less talk about us, how are you doing... really?"

"I'm good." Rosie turned her eyes to Jesse. "Amy comes to see me at least once a week, and they are letting me write. I've finished my last book and have spoken to my agent."

"That's great." Gail took Rosie's hand again. "I wish we could get you out and in time I believe we can."

"Don't fret. Like I said I'm happy here. My agent said my book was the best I've done. Grittier. The money has to go into a trust for now, but it gives me something to do."

"Is it difficult with the other patients?" Jesse let his eyes skip around the room and grimaced at the insensitivity of his words.

"Most of them are not that different. There are a few really disturbed individuals, but they are kept in a more secure area. I've made a few friends."

"That's great." Gail smiled she really was pleased that Rosie was taking this so well. Would she have done the same? She doubted it, but maybe Rosie was right. Having been forced to murder while possessed by an evil spirit must have been far worse than this secure hospital. It looked more like a club than anything and Gail had been surprised that it was mixed. There were male and female prisoners — patients.

"Have you set a date?" Rosie asked.

"We haven't yet, but I wondered about the summer. We're hoping you can come... will be allowed out on license for the wedding. If not we may have it here." Gail laughed as Rosie let out a gasp and then jumped up and pulled her into a hug.

"Have you picked a dress?"

"Not yet, I have it down to a few choices, I can't decide whether to go for a full fairytale or more sleek and modern."

"Stop, stop right now." Jesse held up his hand and got up from the table. "I'm gonna go make us some drinks. I will be five minutes... when I get back, all wedding dress talk must be over."

The girls laughed as he walked away.

"Do you have pictures?" Rosie asked.

"Yeah, and he'll be more than five minutes, so we have time."

Gail pulled a file from her bag. Though she had not been allowed to bring her phone in the guards had let her bring in some pictures. Quickly she spread them all out on the table.

"They are beautiful." Rosie looked at each in turn. "I think the cream ones will go better with your dark hair and complexion."

"I agree." Gail pulled four of the picture away. "Now help me choose."

* * *

JESSE LEFT THE GIRLS TALKING, but instead of heading for the breakroom he signed out of the secure area to check his phone. On a previous visit, Rosie had told them how Shelly and Jack had come to see her and how she was afraid that they would go to RedRise House.

The ghosts of the children had to be dealt with. Sent to peace but it was not proving easy. The owners would not allow them access. Somehow he believed that they knew what the house was. That they knew about the souls of the children stuck there and that they wanted it left that way. Rosie had promised the children she would free them and Gail and Jesse had taken on that promise. They would visit the house, they would release the children with or without the consent of the owners.

What Jesse hadn't told Gail was that he had visited the area and had spoken to a priest there. A man called Nick Aubrey. Jesse knew all about Nick from Rosie, and he had gone against his instincts in asking him for help. Nick had been reluctant, but in the end, he had agreed to keep an eye on the place and let Jesse know if anyone showed up. Of course, he didn't have a phone, not even a landline, so Jesse had left him with one and asked that he call if anyone showed up. At the time he wondered if that were foolish. What if Nick couldn't use the phone?

It looked like it wasn't. Two days ago Nick had left him a stilted message that was drowned out by static.

"Jesse, I don't know if this magic box will get the message to you, I hope and pray it will. I saw the Duncan's at RedRise House. They are the... They are disturbing and would only show themselves if something was about to happen. I will speak into this again as soon as I know more."

Jesse had listened to the message over a hundred times. Each time he hoped to hear more, but it was all to no avail. The message was like a recording of a spirit, but that didn't surprise him. Rosie had told them of her meeting with the priest. How he had written in the book about the house hundreds of years before and how when she tried to find his house she came to a grave.

Jesse knew that Nick was dead he just didn't know if Nick

knew it. The other question that haunted his dreams was whether the priest was on their side or his own. He had a history with the house, and Jesse's instincts told him that the man, spirit, was good but he had been wrong before. A lot was riding on this — he had to believe that Nick's intentions were good for the only alternative was that he was trying to lure them there to give the house even more power.

Taking his phone from the guard, Jesse stepped outside. The breeze was cold but the day was dry. Walking a little way from the building he turned on the phone and saw a notification that he had another message. The little red one kicked his pulse up a notch, and he dialed his voice mail.

"Jesse, Jesse are you there. Jesse, I need to talk to you." The message was lost as a hiss of static burst into his ear.

Pulse racing breath coming in desperate gasps he pressed to play it again. The static was bad, the recording sounded scratchy, but he got no more from the conversation. Looking at the phone, he could see that it was received just fifteen minutes before. Should he call Nick back? He doubted if the priest would know how to answer the phone. Jesse had been careful to get Nick an older phone. One that had buttons and not a touchscreen. Even so, it had taken him over an hour to show him how to make a call.

This left him no choice. They had to visit RedRise House and find out what had happened. As he swiveled on his heels his phone buzzed in his hand. Recognizing the number he quickly swiped and put the phone to his ear.

"Nick is that you?"

"Jesse, can you hear me, Jesse?"

The man's voice was panicked and unsure, and Jesse wanted

to laugh at how difficult the modern world must be to a spirit like Nick. If the circumstances were different, then it would be funny.

"I can hear you, Nick, what have you got for me?"

"I don't understand... before you were talking but not there. What sorcery is this?"

Jesse ran a hand across his hair and tried to curb his impatience. "Don't worry about that. I am here now, tell me what's happening."

"Well I tried to call yesterday, but I couldn't get this contraption to work. It was just not there most of the time."

Jesse understood. Nick was an old spirit, and so he could manipulate the physical world very well, but it would take effort. No doubt most of the time he did that automatically, but if he were worried, panicked, or tired then he would forget, and his hands would pass straight through the phone.

"That is understandable in your circumstances. What did you want to tell me?"

"Yes, yes of course. A young couple arrived at the house. I tried to talk to them. I even went inside, but I couldn't stay. There is evil there, and I fear for the lives of the young couple. They do not know what they are doing, do not know what they have gotten themselves into. Can you help them?"

"I will go straight there. Will the Duncan's be a problem?"

There was silence for a few moments, and Jesse wondered if the spirit had tired himself and faded from this plane, but then he spoke.

"No, they will have expended a lot of energy to lure these people and will need to recuperate. If you come quickly, they will not trouble you. I will try and be there, but I am also tired."

"Thank you, Nick, when this is over I will come and find you and if you wish I will help you move on."

Once more silence descended between them there was just the occasional crackle of static.

"I will not leave until I am sure it is over, I promise you that."

"I promise," Jesse said, and the line dropped, Nick was gone for now.

Now all Jesse had to do was explain to Gail that he had been lying to her for a few months and then get her to come with him to RedRise House. Then he thought about Rosie. He had to hide this from her. Knowing that it wasn't over would hurt her. It might make her feel as if her sacrifice was for nothing. He couldn't do that. As he rushed back, he knew that he might not have a choice. Rosie was clever, she understood the nature of this more than any of them.

CHAPTER 9

"**Y**ou forgot the drinks," Gail said as Jesse came back into the room. "What's wrong?"

"It's nothing, just a client who needs help." Jesse sat down at the table, he couldn't look at Rosie, and he couldn't keep his hands still.

"You don't have to lie to me," Rosie said. "I know it sounds strange... I felt it awaken. Those two amateurs went to the house didn't they?"

Jesse thought about lying. The words curled on his tongue waiting to come out.

Rosie cocked her head to one side, her long brunette hair fell across her shoulders, and as she tensed her jaw, the scar on her left cheek moved. Jessie understood that she knew, and she wouldn't want him to lie.

He nodded.

"How do you know?" Gail asked them both.

"I... I..." Jesse stumbled on how to tell her.

"Jesse tell me." She raised an eyebrow and pinned him to the spot with her big brown eyes.

"I went to see Nick, the priest and got him to pass me a message if anything happened."

"How bad is it?" Rosie's voice was little more than a whisper, but she looked strong.

"They have been at the house since yesterday. I think Nick panicked and couldn't get the phone I left him to work."

"A ghost can use a phone?" Gail asked.

"I wasn't sure." He shrugged. "I thought it was worth a try. Nick has been around so long he is pretty good at controlling the material. I was going to go check myself if I didn't hear from him soon."

"What now?" Gail had already started to stand.

Jesse looked at Rosie. "Did they leave you a phone number?"

"Yes, they did." She reached over and opened a book and scrolled through the pages until she found one with some scribbled notes. In a circle at the top was a phone number. Without hesitating, she tore it out and handed it to Jesse.

"We have to go," he said as he took it. "Don't worry, without the Old Hag they will have time. The house is still dangerous but what you did has saved their lives. If she still lived there, she would have sacrificed them by now and would bind them to her for all eternity."

"You will get rid of it this time," Rosie said. "Promise me that! You will get rid of every last evil molecule of the place. Burn it to the ground if need be."

"We promise," Gail said and then she walked around and hugged Rosie. "We will see you soon and tell you all about it."

"Be safe."

Jesse nodded, and the two of them walked away. He hated how those two words would not leave his mind. Once more he was taking Gail into danger and more than anything he wanted her to be safe. What was he doing?

* * *

THE CORRIDOR WAS dark as Shelly turned onto it, but she didn't notice. Fear snapped at her heels like a rabid dog. It pushed her onward, driving her away from its ferocious teeth. All she could think of was the children. The poor children, the terrible children. She had come here to save them — they wanted to kill her, to keep her here with them. *Where was Jack?* A sob escaped her as she tumbled forward down the never-ending corridor. She had brought Jack here. She had brought him to his death.

With the phone clutched in her hand, she had a little light, but she didn't know where to run. The twin hounds of fear and despair chased her until her legs ached and her lungs screamed for air. But the corridor went on and on. From the light of the phone, all she could see was a few steps in front of her. The light flashing back and forward as she pounded her arms. The crazy flashing light was making her dizzy. Only adrenaline pushed her onward, but the lack of oxygen and despair held her back. And all the time she was chased by the shrill keening of the children's throats.

A shadow passed in front of her. She dug in her heels and ground to a halt as terror turned her blood to ice. Raising the phone, she peered into the darkness. There was nothing there. The noise had stopped. The silence was deafening. Something moved behind her. She spun around, nothing was there. Spinning round and round she searched the darkness with the light of the camera. It showed so little, just a glimpse of a few feet in front of her and the more she turned, the dizzier she became until suddenly she didn't know which way was which.

It made no sense the corridor wasn't this long the house wasn't this big. Was it panic creating this illusion or was it the spirits? Had they gotten into her mind, were they driving her crazy?

Something moved against her leg, and she squealed and jumped back. Pointing the camera at the ground, she let out a hysterical laugh. The cat was there at her side.

"You scared the bejesus out of me."

She bent down and scooped him into her arms. He was still cold, even so, he was a comfort. He purred against her ear as she cuddled him to her face. The contact made her feel instantly better. It calmed her mind and gave her time to think. She knew what she had to do. She would call Gail and Jesse, she would call The Spirit Guides and then she would find Jack.

Taking the phone, she checked the signal and battery. The first was no bars the second said 50% it was enough, but she didn't want to stay here. Not in this freaky long corridor with the children behind, or in front of her. The first thing she needed to do was find out which way she was pointing. She almost laughed at the absurdity of it. The cat purred in her arms.

"Come on kitty, we'll find Jack, then we'll get you out of here.

Taking the phone off camera, she turned on the touch app and shone it down the corridor. Relief washed over her and filled her eyes with tears as she saw the door to the bedroom just in front of her and the end of the corridor not far after that. Turning around she shone the other way, and sure enough, the corridor opened out into the hallway.

"You must be my lucky kitty, come on let's go find Jack."

As she set off toward the hallway, the lights came back on. Quickly she turned off the touch app and rushed down the corridor.

The sound of her feet on the hardwood floor was now reassuring, normal and she welcomed any sound that wasn't the keening children.

The hallway opened up before her and she wanted to run up the stairs but she instead she rushed to the front door. The key was in the lock, but it wouldn't turn. It was to be expected. When Rosie had told them that the house wouldn't let her leave Shelly had thought she was simply panicking. That she was inexperienced and scared of things, she didn't understand. Shelly believed it wouldn't happen to her but then she had believed the children would welcome her and would talk to her and pass a message onto her sister before she finally sent them to peace.

She kicked the door and pulled as hard as she could, it wouldn't budge. For a moment she was swamped with feelings of inadequacy, stupidity, and foolish naïveté. Did she really believe she could handle the spirits? Of course, she had, but that was before, now she just hoped that she got out of here with her life and more importantly with Jack's life. Tears flooded her eyes, she wanted to curl up on the floor and wail out her despair. "Stop it!"

She had got them into this, she had to be brave enough to get them out... or at least to try.

The cat wriggled in her arms, but she held on tight and smoothed his coat to placate him. Having the creature gave her company, confidence, it kept her able to think. If he was to disappear, she didn't know if she could cope.

Balancing him against her hip, she scrolled through the contacts on her phone until she found the number for The Spirit Guide. Though she wouldn't tell anyone, she had watched Gail and Jesse's career with interest. Finding out everything she could about them. What they did intrigued and fascinated her. On the outside, she had always believed that she was as good as them — if she was just given a chance. Now she wondered if she would ever get the chance to tell them how much she admired them.

She had to stop thinking like this. She had to find Jack.

The logical place to search was upstairs. That was the last place she had seen him. Like a hero, he had pushed her in front of him. Something must have happened as she raced down the stairs full of excitement. What a fool she had been.

The lights flickered and dimmed for a moment. As she was plunged into darkness, fear squeezed her heart like a fist clamping on tightly. It froze the blood in her veins. For a moment she thought she would faint. Wobbling she reached out and steadied herself against the door. The cat meowed in her arms and struggled. She couldn't lose him. Taking a deep breath, she calmed herself as much as she could. Listening, feeling in the dark for danger, for anything. As her mind calmed, the lights came back on.

For a moment she wondered, were the spirits feeding on her fear? When she controlled herself things got better. The more afraid she was the worst they became. There again, maybe that was just life in general.

Quickly she dialed the phone, but it flashed up no signal. She moved to the side and tried again. Raising the phone into the air, she tried again. It was no use there was no signal, but there was one way that might work. Quickly she typed out a text explaining where she was and what was happening she asked for their help. She pressed send praying the text would go. It wouldn't there was still no signal. It didn't matter, fingers crossed, sometime soon it would get a signal and help would be on the way. Until then she had to find Jack.

Feeling more confident Shelly called out, "Jack, Jack where are you?"

The words echoed around the empty house coming back to mock her. Part of Shelly wanted to keep quiet, wanted to sneak around the house without the spirits knowing where she was but she knew that was ridiculous. They lived here, looking at their clothes they had been here for many generations, and they were on a different plane. There was no way she could hide from them, whether she made noise or didn't, it wouldn't matter to them... it might matter to Jack.

"Jack, hold on I'm coming for you. If you can give me a sign, do so, but if not I will find you... I promise."

Holding the cat snuggly against her side she set off for the stairs. That was when she noticed that the rope had been pulled back across. Jack had taken it down when they first went up there. It had been down when she ran past only now it was back up. Blocking her way. If only they had listened to the Duncan's, and not gone upstairs, then maybe none of this would have happened.

That didn't matter it was too late for what-ifs now, all she could do was find Jack and get the hell out of here.

Unhooking the rope, she let it drop to the stairs. The heavy metal clip made hardly a sound as it sank into the thick carpet. Without hesitating, she walked past. Slowly but confidently she made her way up the stairs. She still held the phone in front of her, the camera on, recording everything that happened. This was no longer an adventure, but she still felt it was important that she document as much as she could. After all, the phone would be there even if she and Jack weren't.

This time she ignored how the carpet changed as she climbed the stairs. It was immaterial. Part of her understood that the house was decaying, that it was only kept in a livable state by the energy of the spirits. That it was probably much worse than it appeared but she didn't need to think of that now, all she needed to do was find Jack.

When she got to the top of the stairs, her heart sank. There at the side was the discarded torch, still on, and shining at the paint peeling from the wall.

"Jack, Jack where are you. Please just give me a sign."

Shelly turned around looking down both lengths of the corridor. Hoping for a sign, hoping for anything to tell her where he had gone. And then she saw it.

There were clear signs that somebody had been dragged across the carpet. Dragged down the hallway toward the room with the piano. There were deep scuff marks, where the rotted carpet had been pulled up and torn. Fear squeezed her chest and raised the hairs on her arms. As she stared at the carpet the light at the end of the corridor started to fade. Once more the corridor was longer than it should be and

Jack was somewhere down there. Down that never-ending corridor. Did she have the courage to find him?

All around her came the sound of whispers. Sibilant sounds just at the edge of her hearing. She turned around, no one was there.

A scream came shrill in the night behind her.

She whipped around causing the cat to meow in her arm. With the phone held up as a weapon she let out a sigh of relief. No one was there. The lights dimmed more and more, she was plunged into darkness.

Had the scream been Jacks?

* * *

OUTSIDE THE HOUSE, Nick stood in the darkness and watched as the lights flicked on and off, on and off. He could hear the whispers like the rustling of leaves on the trees or the crack of a stick in the forest behind him. They were threatening sounds, the sounds of a predator prowling, waiting, and planning. They sapped the strength from his bones and the courage from his heart. For a moment he turned around, this was not his fight, not anymore, maybe it was time to let go. Slowly he started to walk away, as he did, he became less substantial. Less visible. He knew that if he kept going soon he would be nothing but mist and there would be nothing, no one, to help the young couple.

Ignoring his fear, he turned back and walked slowly toward the house. He doubted he could get in this door, doubted he could do much to help, but he would be here waiting, watching as he had always done.

* * *

JESSE KNEW that Gail was angry with him. Mad because he had kept this from her, he also knew that she was excited and scared in equal measures.

"You should have told me," she said her arms crossed as she stared out the windscreen. Jesse was driving as fast as he could but it was hard to concentrate, and it would soon be dark. The chances are it was already dark at RedRise House. Things happen differently in a haunted property, time behaved differently, the couple would be scared, and he didn't doubt they were in danger.

"I know I should have... I didn't think they would get in. From everything I've read the owners of the house can't be found. With Matron gone it seemed foolish to believe that there would be much danger."

Gail laughed. "I guess we've made that mistake a time or two." She raised her eyebrows at him and gave him a smile.

Jesse nodded but turned his eyes back to the road.

"I promise, I'm never gonna say, *this will be an easy job*, again."

Gail laughed. "You do have a habit of jinxing them."

"I guess we should have visited the house before now. We knew there was activity there, we knew those kids needed peace. Maybe we should have made the time sooner."

"Yes maybe we should, but who would we have let down if we did? Margie, Mark, Donna, Joe, Paul, or Philip? These are all the people we have helped with genuine hauntings never mind all the ones that we've put their minds to rest because they weren't being haunted. We were going to get to the house, but the priority has to be where lives are at risk and from what we knew they weren't, not at RedRise, not then. So don't be feeling guilty for things we can't change. We know what's happening now... let's go there... let's help these two and then let's put those children to rest."

"Thanks, I needed that. Did I ever tell you how clever you are and how much I love you?"

"Ermmmm, now let me think... maybe you did once or twice, but I'm not gonna stop you doing it again."

She reached across and rubbed his shoulder. "It won't take us long to get there will it?"

"About another hour."

Gail sighed. "I hate to say this, but my gut tells me we need to hurry."

Jesse nodded and put his foot down a little harder on the accelerator. The roads were difficult, he had to be careful, but Gail was right they needed to hurry.

CHAPTER 10

*S*helly froze in the darkness and bit back a sob. Why had she come here? Why had she been so foolish?

The whispers surrounded her — they hissed like a wind of lies and deceit and came from every possible direction. She turned one way and the other trying to find the source of the sound, but it moved. It was always behind her. As she spun, she could swear she felt the splash of spittle on her neck. Batting at the air, she turned again. The whisper was so close. She felt the touch of lips on her ear. Hands flapping around her head, the phone caused sparks of light but showed nothing clearly. It was just a flash here and a flash there, showing shadows and empty corridors and so much darkness for something to hide in.

Turning and turning the panic rose inside her like a volcano bubbling to escape. As it reached its crescendo, her knees gave way. She sank to the floor. The carpet was damp, moist, and cold but she didn't care. Hugging the cat close to her she rocked and cried. Despite the fact that she had never been religious she prayed that she would escape this evil place. She prayed for Jack. How she wanted him there, wanted him next to her. Wanted to tell him how she felt and how stupid she was for putting him in danger. Only it was no use, she would die here. Jack was probably already dead.

Tears ran from her eyes and dripped down onto her hands. They were warm, and something about them gave her resolve.

The cat meowed again. Did it understand? Was it encouraging her to pull herself out of this? Shaking her head, she bit back the tears and swallowed. The whispers were still there, like rustling leaves in the lonely forest. She couldn't make out the words — it was like somebody trying to hide what they were saying.

"Shut up," she shouted into the darkness. "I came to help you. If you won't help me then shut up and get out of my way."

Putting the hand with the phone in it on the moist floor she gritted her teeth against the revulsion it caused. The carpet felt like wet skin that was skidding across bones. Forcing that thought from her mind, she pushed herself to her feet. Taking a long deep breath, she tried to still her heart. To calm the rushing blood that raced through her ears and drowned out all coherent thought. Nothing had changed, nothing could hurt her, she had to keep that in mind and search for Jack. That was all that counted.

"Jack. I'm coming for you, please just give me a sign." The words echoed down the hallway, and the gloom lifted a little. She could see a few feet in front of her. Just at the edge of her vision, there were shadows. Misty shapes moved in and out of her field-of-view. There was nothing solid about them but occasionally she could spot a figure in the darkness. Then a face would appear contorted into a scream. Forcing herself to stay calm, to not jump, she walked toward the figures.

"Like I said, helped me, or get out of my way."

The figures faded away, and the lights came back on. It was darker than it had been but she could see clearly. The corridor stretched out before her disappearing into the distance.

Her mind knew that couldn't be right. It had to be an optical illusion caused by the spirits, but it didn't matter, she could see. If she could see, she could find Jack.

Taking a shaky breath, she set off toward the room with the piano. The door had slammed in their face when they had heard the scream downstairs. She could see it was back open and she hoped that Jack would be there.

The door swung toward her as she approached it. Without thinking she put out her arm to stop it slamming shut. It touched her with some force but not enough to hurt, and she pushed it open again and peered inside. The piano stood there all alone. Just a relic, with chipped paint and moldy woodwork all alone in the center of a bare room.

Shelly pushed the door back even further and glanced inside there was nothing there, no one there. Disappointment was like lead on her shoulders, it didn't matter, it was time to move on.

Pulling the door closed behind her she walked down the corridor to the next door which was on her right. It was open. She peered inside. As she did the temperature dropped, and her breath streamed out before her. She knew what this meant, spirit activity. It wasn't going to stop her, it wasn't going to make her fear, not now, not this time. This room was bigger, and she couldn't see it all from the doorway. As she tried to cross the threshold, the cat struggled in her arms leaping to the floor and darting away.

"Dammit no."

For a moment she hesitated in the doorway. The loss of the creature was a blow to her, but there was more. The cat was frightened of this room and so should she be. Letting out a sigh she almost laughed — she should be afraid of the whole damn house. Taking another long deep breath, she stepped into the room and noticed that it was even colder. It didn't matter, she crossed behind the door and looked around the mainly barren room. There was some furniture an old wardrobe, a bed that had seen better days. They were surrounded by darkness.

"Jack are you in there?"

Stilling her breath, she listened for any sign that he might be here. There was nothing, Even the whispers had stopped. Somehow the silence was even worse, but she shook it off and walked toward the door. Darkness coalesced there swirled swarming and swirling, and she was frightened to approach, but something else scared her more.

The bed, what was beneath or behind the bed?

She didn't know why but she felt that something hid there. That something dark was waiting and that once she approached it, all would be lost. The fear was so great that she froze on the spot, her legs wouldn't move, though she wanted to turn and run all she could do was stand there shaking.

"Stop this, dammit stop this."

Hearing her own voice helped and she took a step. As she did the shadow became more substantial it was a figure bigger than the children? This had to be an adult. One of the ones that were holding the children? She remembered the tales that Rosie had told of Matron. Fear was like a beast holding her back, crushing her down, forcing her knees to be weak, and her arms to fail. Only she wouldn't let it, she came here, it was her choice, and she would see this through.

"Get out of my way, or I will send you back to the hell you came from."

The sound of laughter wafted through the air behind her. She spun around. There was nothing there, no one there, as she turned back the mist had formed into the solid shape of a figure. Covered in a dark, heavy robe, the head bowed so she couldn't see the face beneath the hood.

Her heart froze and missed a beat as the figure ran toward her throwing back its head. The hood fell away, and she let out a scream.

Beneath the hood was a skull the mouth twisted into a grimace of death.

Shelly tried to step back away, but her body wouldn't move, all she could do was close her eyes and brace for impact.

* * *

JACK JERKED awake to the sound of chanting. Where was he? What had happened?

Flickering light did little to chase away the darkness. Shadows loomed across the stone walls like monsters stalking the perimeter. This was not the corridor he had been in. The room was too big and felt different, it felt like a cave. Fear sent a shockwave through him raising the hairs on his arms and tripling his heart rate. Terrified his head flicked left and right but no one was there.

He tried to sit up but his head ached, and his body felt bruised and battered. A wave of nausea had him slumping back down onto something hard and cold.

It felt like stone beneath him. Instinct told him he had to move and he tried to sit up again. The room spun, just like the time he drank too much and couldn't get off the bed, he was forced to lay back down. For a moment he closed his eyes and listened. The sound of the chanting was getting closer. He couldn't understand what it was but thought it was Latin. Something about it turned his blood to ice and made him think of all the things he meant to do. Shelly, why hadn't he asked her out?

There was no time for regrets, he had to get away before whoever was doing that chanting got here.

Once again he tried to sit, there was less pain, less nausea, but it was still too much. He flopped back down like a drunk or a rag doll. There was no substance to his body, and for now, it wouldn't support him.

Moving his hands, he explored the surface beneath him. It felt like a stone bench. The thought flashed through his mind, a picture from one of the movies that Shelly loved so much, of him lying on a sacrificial altar waiting for some occult priestess to offer him in supplication to a dark presence.

He pushed the picture aside, it left behind fear and desolation. Then he thought about Shelly. Where was she? Was she safe? Would she escape from here? It was enough to drive him to try again, and this time he managed to sit up. The pounding in his head compared to a jackhammer but he bit down on the bile that filled his throat and closed his eyes for a moment. The room stopped spinning or at least slowed down.

He swung his legs over the side and found his feet just reached the floor. It was too soon to stand, but it gave him a better view of the room.

They were four flaming torches, one on each wall. They cast little light and created shadows that bounced and flashed like gargoyles and demons hunting him down. Maybe this was just his imagination, maybe he was lying in the corridor, and maybe this was all a dream.

Something... sweat, was running down his neck and he reached up to find it was warm and slick. Blood. That had to be what the pain in his head was. Tentatively he searched with his fingers. They found matted, sticky hair and at the back of his head, he could feel a large lump and a gash within it.

A burst of fear flooded his arms with prickly heat and filled his stomach with grease. What if he needed stitches? There was no time to worry about that, no time for anything, for the chanting was getting closer and closer, somehow he knew that once they arrived, it was over for him.

The sound of footsteps on concrete could be heard below the chanting. Part of him wanted to shout at them to go away, to shut up, to leave him alone and part of him just wanted to run, but he couldn't even stand?

He guessed it was time to try, so he eased himself along the bench. It was scratchy and cold against his butt and legs. He ignored the discomfort and the wave of nausea, hitching forward until his feet were more solidly on the floor. Using his hands to lever, he took his weight and was pleasantly surprised that his knees didn't buckle beneath him.

The chanting was getting closer. He had to move now. Quickly he checked his pockets, there was no phone, and he had dropped the torch in the corridor. There had to be doors to this room, had to be a way to escape but he couldn't see it. So he staggered away from the table toward the closest flame.

The flickering light was disconcerting. It flashed before his eyes creating darkness and light that was hard to see through, but it was all he had.

When he reached the wall, he pulled the torch from the sconce it was resting in and held it above him. Another wave of nausea buckled his knees. Biting down on his lip steadied him. He had to stay upright. Had to get out of here before... before they arrived and it was too late. There was one door that he could see directly to his right. The only problem was the chanting and footsteps were coming from that direction.

Holding the light out in front of him, he stumbled across the room searching for another exit. Searching for anything. For somewhere to hide, for some way of escape but there was nothing to see. The room looked like it had been carved out of rock and he imagined it was underneath the house. He walked to the furthest wall and put his hand on it. It was cold and slick with water but it was solid, there was no way through. If this was a dream it was realistic so how could he get out of here?

Bit by bit he circumnavigated the edge of the room, looking for something anything that could help him. The only thing he had was the torch. Maybe he could use it as a weapon, maybe he could escape by hitting the intruders when they came but there sounded like a lot of them, and his strength was already fading.

He had the urge to sit down and to let them come. Maybe even to go back to the altar and to lie in wait. Then this would be over, and he could rest. Only he couldn't do that, he couldn't let Shelly down. She was out there alone and terrified. He had to save her.

Inspired and given new strength he walked further around the dark, dank room, looking, searching, hoping for anything to help but there was nothing. Then he heard a hand on the door and knew that his captors were here, knew that his life would soon be over. Turning he faced the door with the torch as his only weapon, he wouldn't go down easily.

As the door opened more torches came in carried by two figures in dark cloaks behind them were a number of children their heads were down. They looked dirty and solemn, he got the sudden urge to help them. Maybe these were the children Shelly had spoken about. The ones she wanted to free, the ones Rosie had promised she would free. Would they help him? It didn't matter he couldn't risk it, letting out a scream of anguish he ran toward them waving the torch through the air. Like a murmur of swallows, they moved out to surround him.

The flame whooshed as he parried, creating crazy shadows and bringing his dizziness back to full force. He hit the adults first expecting a kickback as the torch thrashed into their bodies, but it never came. The flame went straight through the figures He stumbled forward as the torch went through them, they were insubstantial, they couldn't hurt him, and so he ran on. Head down giving everything he got he swung the torch in front of them as he charged at the group.

He expected to dive straight through and to run on down the hallway only this time the torch was yanked from his fingers and floated off into the air.

"No," he screamed, but it was too late, for though he ran as fast as he could his feet were no longer on the floor and he was getting nowhere. The children threw back their heads, he could see the terrible wounds at their throats as they started to make an inhuman keening sound.

Something held him high above the ground — suspended — paralyzed. The children circled around him. Though he tried to fight to thrash his arms and feet, to roll his head and body, he couldn't move. Paralysis held him perfectly still except for his racing heart and the bead of sweat that ran down his cheek to drip onto the floor. Inaction and immobility heightened the feat until he thought that his heart would burst.

Gently he was carried across the air with the children walking beneath him they circled the altar, and he was placed down on top of it.

The two robed adults appeared on either side of his head, and then he saw the knife. And he started to scream.

CHAPTER 11

*S*helly braced for impact. It was just a fraction of a second, but she closed her eyes and clenched her fists and waited. Every part of her knew that this was the end and yet her life didn't flash before her. Instead, she saw Jack's sweet face. Saw him blushing and knowing how she felt, now it was too late. She had killed him, killed them both.

The spirit hit her. There was nothing but cold. A cold, disturbing feeling as the spirit passed right through. Shaking, dropping to her knees she scrambled around on the floor to see him behind her.

"Get up," she shouted and hauled herself to her feet.

Though her heart pounded and her knees were weak she was filled with a feeling of power. She had faced it down, it... he couldn't hurt her. Now all she had to do was send him away. She knew many banishing rituals, had even brought a book of them here, but hadn't managed to read it. It didn't matter, she wanted to use the one that Rosie had used when she was trapped here. None of the ones

Shelly knew had ever been tried. They were just words on a page. Rosie had done this with no knowledge. She had survived this house when Matron was here, Shelly was determined to survive too. She wouldn't give up, not even on Jack there was more of the house to search. She would search it, she would find him, and they would get out of here.

So what was the releasing ritual? The more she searched her mind, the more elusive it became, and she knew she didn't have long.

The air was freezing, her breath misted before her face, and her arms were covered in goosebumps. The spirit stood, his hands at his side, his head down hiding that awful skull.

What was the ritual? "I rebuke you." *No that wasn't it.* "In the name of the Lord," her voice was shaky and unsure.

The spirit raised his head only this time the skull was gone, she recognized him. It was the old man. The white hair was hidden by the hood, but she would never forget those eyes. Cold, dark, they filled her with despair. This was the one who had welcomed her here. It was Mr. Duncan. Had he tricked her? Had he known she would be stuck here, he must have. Where was the woman?

Once more she tried to think of the ritual, it just wouldn't come to her mind. Everything was happening so quickly, and she just kept worrying about Jack.

Shelly felt the grey-haired man's eyes on her. Like insects pattering all over her arms, they made her skin crawl. That wasn't as bad as the look he gave her. Those dark, desolate eyes bored into her soul and saw only the worst. Beneath his gaze, she felt shallow, foolish, inexperienced, and naïve. They made her out to be nothing, and she shrank beneath their black hated stare.

This seemed to please him, for the first time, he smiled. It was not a nice smile but one that could curdle milk and crush children.

At first, it had the required effect, pushing her back, crushing her down. Shaking her head she fought against it, she was made of more than this, he had no right. He had no right to trick her, no right to judge her. At last, the ritual came to her mind. "In the Name of Jesus, I rebuke the spirit..."

Rage crossed his face and once more he flew at her. In the blink of an eye, he crossed the distance between them becoming incorporeal for just a moment. As he re-materialized wind rose in the hallway and Shelly was blasted off her feet and sent tumbling down the corridor.

Her back hit a door frame, and she crashed to a halt bruised, battered, and disoriented. But the pain sparked her anger. She clawed herself back to her feet. That was when she remembered something that Rosie had said. It was not the words of the exorcism or the releasing prayer that were as important as the intention. So far her intention had been fear and escape, that wouldn't do. So she clenched her fists so hard that her nails dug into her palms and with all her heart she wanted this spirit gone.

"In the Name of Jesus Christ, I rebuke the spirit of Clive Duncan."

The spirit roared and rushed toward her but she stepped lightly aside, and that was when she saw the bottle of Holy Water. Somewhere along the way she had lost her own but there was Jack's lying, unbroken, and waiting for her. She stepped to the side and scooped it up. Without stopping she turned around so that she was behind the spirit and unscrewed the top. Before he realized what she was doing, she threw half the bottle over him.

Clive roared with rage and turned toward her. Smoke rose in silky tendrils from his cloak, and suddenly he was not as intimidating.

Pulling himself to his full height and throwing back his head he showed her the skull once more.

Only Shelly was no longer terrified, afraid yes, wary, sure, but she was more determined, more angry. She was having none of it. She had nothing to lose and everything to fight for, so she advanced toward him and saw him shimmer slightly.

"You not so sure now, are you?"

The wind rose in the corridor swirling around her pushing, pulling, shoving but she held her feet and held her ground. Another step toward him and she splashed more Holy Water and watched with delight as it sizzled on his cloak.

"In the Name of Jesus Christ, I rebuke the spirit of Clive Duncan." The name had come to her the first time she said the words and this time she knew what she wanted from the releasing prayer. She wanted this beast gone from this place, from her sight. She wanted him back in the hell he came from.

"I command you leave this place, without manifestation and without harm to me or anyone..."

Before her, he began to fade. At first simply becoming more translucent. It filled her with a power she could not believe. Though she had always wanted to do this, up until now, it had always been make-believe. Just a childish dream but nothing real. Now she understood, she had the power, she could get rid of spirits, and she would do. Taking one more step toward him, she held out the bottle of Holy Water as a threat.

The spirit shrank before her and disappeared in the blink of an eye.

If only she had done this before, if only. She knew the power of the releasing ritual, it didn't matter... he was gone, and there were more important things to do. She had to find Jack.

Taking a moment to catch a breath and savor what just happened Shelly looked down the corridor. It was short and had shrunk back to the normal size that it should be. There were four doors on each side in front of her and four on each side behind her. So far she had checked just two of them. Now she would search the rest, the third floor, the rest of the house, and she would find Jack.

Quickly she ran to the next door and pushed it open. It was an empty room filled with eight wooden bunk beds. There were stains on the walls, stains on the wooden floor and the room felt desolate and full of despair. Bad things had happened here. Was this where the children were hurt, where they were murdered? Clive had said they weren't murdered here and had put emphasis on the here. She had been a fool, he meant the spot they had been standing on, not the house.

She stood for a few moments longer than she should have, there was something about the room that made her want to stay.

"I'm here to help you, will you help me?"

A gentle breeze swirled around her hair lifting her ponytail and tickling her neck. It was warm and smelt of summer flowers and was nothing like the wind she had felt before. Maybe now it was time for a dialogue.

So she stood and listened and waited... nothing else happened. Turning she closed the door and ran to the next one.

This room was much like the last one filled with bunk beds. Sat on the top of one at the back of the room was a young girl. Leaning against the wall she had her knees up and her arms around them, her head relaxed forward. The sound of sobbing came from the room, and Shelly was filled with sadness.

"Hello, my name's Shelly, I'm here to help you... what is your name?"

The sobbing continued and filled her with such despair that it crushed her chest. Shelly took a step toward her but as she did the girl faded away.

"No, no don't go, don't leave me."

A final sob filled the air and then there was nothing but silence.

Shelly could breathe once more, she wanted to stay there, wanted to try and communicate, but she knew that time was short. So she walked over to the bed and put a hand on the dirty blanket where the girl had been sat. It was cold, damp, and as she pulled her hand away, it was covered in blood.

Shelly let out a scream and stepped back rubbing her hand. When she looked again her hand was clean, there had been no blood — it was just an illusion.

She left the room, closed the door and continue down to the next one.

As she approached the door, she could hear the sound of whispers and the hair rose on the back of her neck. Part of her wanted to run, but she had to know. The sibilant sounds continued, harsher now and more threatening, but still she would not turn back. She pushed the door open, a shadow crossed in front of her. The air was cold, her breath frosted in front of her and shadows moved across the furthest corner.

"I'm here to help you. To give you peace. Will you help me first?"

The whispers rose and fell in the air. Though she couldn't hear the words, the tone was angry, and a strong wind rose in the room. It filled her nose and clogged her throat with the scent of decay. Swallowing bile, she ignored the smell of something long dead and opened her arms. In response, the wind hit her hard and pushed her back to the corridor. The door slammed, and the air was filled with cruel laughter.

Shelly tried to control her breathing, but it was difficult. Taking gasp after gasp, she calmed herself as much as she could and turned toward the next door.

She waited outside and listened, there was nothing to hear. Opening the door, she found nothing but an empty room. Dark stains marred the painted walls. It looked like it had once been white but was now a horrible cream covered in what she knew to be blood.

As she turned to leave she saw a young boy peeking his head around the next door. He smiled and beckoned for her to come to him and suddenly she was filled with hope.

CHAPTER 12

*J*ack was lying on the altar surrounded by children and three adults in heavy cloaks. The children's heads were down their eyes sad for they knew what was coming. Somehow he knew this was where they had died. That they had lain here afraid, terrified, and that someone, probably one of these three had ended their lives.

Though his own fear was beyond his control a part of him felt for them, and another part could think of nothing but Shelly. Would she blame herself? He knew she would. That was her, always thinking of others and more than anything he hoped she didn't find him.

The chanting began again, it was Latin, he couldn't understand any of it, somehow that made it worse.

Two adults stood at his shoulders facing him, the third one stood at his feet. Their heads were bowed, the hoods covering their faces and he was afraid to see them. Afraid of what was beneath the dark material of those hoods.

The children spread around in a circle, and all joined hands.

"Let me out of here," Jack shouted. "Just let me the hell out of here. I won't tell anyone what you've done."

The only answer was a shrill keening sound. It started low, just on the edge of his hearing, and yet it scraped across his nerves like a bow across a badly tuned string. Gradually the noise increased in volume until it filled the room and sapped away his strength. What was he to do? How could he get out of here?

"There is no way," a deep, gruff voice said. "We lost her, the one we worship, maybe if we take enough souls she will return to us."

The words chilled Jack to the bone. They were not just going to kill him they were going to keep him here, like these children, forever. Maybe they would even force him to kill, just like Rosie had been forced to kill.

The children walked clockwise around him. He tried to watch, tried to struggle, but the adults clasped hold of him. One on each shoulder one on his legs. No matter how hard he tried, though he bucked, kicked, and rolled his body, they kept him pinned to the hard cold stone. Bony fingers dug into his flesh so hard that he knew they would bruise and still he kicked and fought but it was all to no avail.

Round and round the children went and he found he was watching with them praying they kept moving because somehow he knew when they stopped it was time. They changed direction and circled the opposite way.

"Help me, please help me," he called into the darkness, it was of no use. No one was listening, no one was helping him, he would die here tonight. Die by the knife that he had seen earlier where was it now?

As if in answer to his question the cloaked figure next to him pulled the knife from beneath his cloak and held it high above him. It caught the light of the flames and flashed orange light like the fires of hell.

Fear knelt on his chest like a sumo wrestler forcing the air from his lungs and crushing his spirit. Tears fell from his eyes and ran down his face to land on the cold stone.

This was it.

The children stopped and turned to face him. Jack knew it was coming. This was it his time. What could he do, how could he save himself, how could he escape?

He didn't have the Holy Water he didn't know the rituals, didn't know anything. What was he doing here?

The keening noise still filled the room and one by one the children raised their heads until they were looking up at the ceiling.

Jack let out a scream when he saw what was making the terrible, ear-splitting noise. Ugly, bleeding, crusty and repulsive gashes marred all their throats. All of them were different. Each wound was long and deep. Some showed bone, some just flesh. They moved like obscene mouths, ragged lips flapping as the sound went past them.

They had lain here on this stone bench, on this altar, and sometime, many years ago, that knife had ripped out their lives.

Now it was his turn.

* * *

SHELLY WALKED toward the young boy slowly and calmly. Putting a smile on her face, she tucked the Holy Water in the back of her jeans and showed him that her hands were empty.

He smiled a sweet, cheeky grin that lit up his dirty face.

It was hard to tell what he looked like, but she imagined he was around six years old. However, he was thin and covered in dirt and looks could be deceptive. Blond hair was matted to his head and stuck out in places, but he had rosy lips and sweet eyes.

"I'm here to help you," she said as she got closer and closer. "Can you help me?"

A light laugh floated across the air between them, and he nodded, turned, and disappeared into the room.

Disappointment flooded through her but maybe he just wanted her to follow, and so she did.

As Shelly got to the door, it swung shut toward her, she put out her foot to stop it closing. It jarred right up her leg and crushed her toes, she pushed it open.

The lights dimmed, going off for a moment, and then coming back on but not to full strength. The room was dull, filled with shadows and cold so very cold. She peered across the threshold, she couldn't see the boy hidden within the gloom.

That same light laughter trickled across the air. It was such a happy sound, one that she couldn't be afraid of. Without another thought, she entered the room.

"Are you there?"

Another trickle of laughter.

"I want to help you, but I'm in a hurry to know where my friend is?"

He is in the bad place. The words were spoken in her mind in the voice of a young boy.

"Can you help me find him?"

Then she saw the child, sat in the corner, an old wooden top spinning on the floor before him. His eyes wouldn't leave it as it twirled slower and slower before falling with a clatter to the rotted floorboards. As it stopped, she could see it was crudely made and wondered if the boy had carved it himself.

"I like your toy," she said and moved closer toward him. "May I sit and play with you?"

He looked up at her, and a big smile came on his dirty face. A grubby hand picked up the piece of wood and handed it to her.

It was cold in her fingers and heavier than she expected. Every fiber of her knew she should be looking for Jack knew he didn't have much time, but this boy was her only lead, and part of her also knew she was meant to be here.

Placing the wooden toy on the ground, she spun it, faster, harder than this weakened child was able.

His big eyes were wide in his face, and he clapped his hands with delight. Only there was no sound, and that seemed to make him sad. Picking up the top he nodded to her and then walked through the wall.

Shelly's heart was beating so fast. Part of it was exhilaration, the thrill of meeting a spirit and the joy of seeing him smile. But another part of her was terrified for Jack, did the boy want her to follow him? Would he lead her to Jack or was this just another dead end?

Quickly she got up and sprinted to the door, there he was in the corridor, fainter now. She could see the walls through him, could see the corridor behind him. And she noticed the air was getting warmer. Did that mean he was going? If he did, she'd better hurry.

"Take me to Jack, please."

He nodded and turned to walk toward the stairs. As he got to the top he turned again and smiled at her, then he beckoned with his hand and stepped onto the stairwell.

There were about 15 feet between them, Shelly ran so that she could keep him in her view, but when she got there, he was gone. She spun around looking this way and that way. Down the corridors and then back down the stairs but he was nowhere to be found.

"Where are you? Where did you go?"

There was no answer just the empty corridor. Once more the lights dimmed. Going down so low that it was almost dark.

Shelly's heart pounded against her chest, her knees were weak. Fatigue, worry, despair weighed down heavily on her, and once more she was unsure what to do. Then she heard a sound scraping along the corridor in front of her.

Looking up she saw a young girl. The girl's head was down, long brown hair hung over her shoulders. It was dirty and tangled as was the apron that covered her dress. The hem was tatty around her ankles and showed her dirty bare feet. She had a stick that she was scraping along the floor.

"I'm Shelly can you help me?"

The girl looked up, she looked like she could be twelve years old, much older than the boy, but still thin and dirty. There was no smile on her face, and her eyes were cold and cynical. Much too bitter for one so young.

This way, once more the words were in her head.

The girl turned and walked down the corridor dragging her stick in the opposite direction that Shelly had been searching.

Part of Shelly wanted to run down the stairs. To see if she could find the boy. He was much more welcoming, much less scary, and yet he had gone, and the girl was here. Knowing in her heart that time was limited she had to follow the girl.

As she set off she watched the girl, she would walk so far scraping her stick alone the carpet and then she would flicker out of existence, appearing a little further down the corridor. Every now and then she turned and looked to check that Shelly was following, but there was no smile or warmth in her eyes and Shelly wondered if she was being led to her doom.

The girl was gone again Shelly stopped. Should she follow? Her knees were weak her breath was coming in desperate gasps, and the sense of panic was growing stronger and stronger by the second. But if she didn't follow where would she go? There were still rooms downstairs to be searched, but there were still rooms up here, and on the next floor to be searched. In the end, it was quicker to search these first, so she walked down the corridor as confidently as she could.

The girl flickered into existence right at the end, she turned and looked at one door, and then disappeared.

Shelly followed, but the closer she got to the door the colder it became, and the air was filled with the stench of decay. This could not be good. She wanted to turn around but what if Jack was here? What if he needed her help?

She stood before the door the girl had disappeared through. It was closed, she reached out to turn the handle. For a moment nothing happened, it was firm in her hand, and she couldn't move it. She was so close to turning around, but with one more try the handle moved, and she pushed the door open.

The air was fetid and cold, and it was even darker inside the room. But she stepped in without hesitation reaching for her phone to provide some light.

The door slammed shut behind her.

Shelly dropped the phone and turned to grab the handle. It was so dark. Something moved behind her. Footsteps, dragging across the wooden floor. They were close, too close.

In panic, her hands flailed at the door. Searching for the handle but she couldn't find it. Her fingers scraped across the wood, breaking a nail and bruising the ends but she didn't feel a thing. The thing behind her moved closer and closer.

No matter how much she searched, she couldn't find the handle. She was trapped here, trapped with whatever was hiding in the darkness.

CHAPTER 13

*O*nce outside of the secure hospital and with their phones back in their possession Jesse dialed the number that Shelly and Jack had left. The phone rang and rang before eventually going to voicemail.

"You reached Shelly, leave me some love at the tone." The message was so upbeat it seemed surreal.

"They're not answering, we will keep trying."

Gail nodded, her shoulders were stiff, and she didn't look him in the eye. She was still angry.

It didn't take them long to prepare. The Jeep was packed with everything they needed. All of it packed away neatly in its own compartment, and all ready to go.

"I know you're angry with me," he said as he slammed the back door. "I really didn't think the house was a problem."

Gail opened the passenger door and turned to look at him. "I understand, but you need to trust me more. We work together now, this is our business, and the decisions should be made as a team."

Jesse nodded. "I know... I just thought... I thought you would think I was paranoid." He shrugged.

Gail laughed and gave him a big smile that told him the argument was forgotten. "I know you're paranoid," she said with a wink before jumping into the car and closing the door.

Jesse ran around to the driver's side and climbed in with a big grin on his face. Though he knew they were going into danger, he was also stoked for the possibilities and for the good they could do. This was a real situation. The young Ghost Hunters needed them but more than that, so did the children, who were trapped there. How he wished they could have freed them before this happened, but then, hindsight was a wonderful thing.

Turning the jeep away from the hospital they took the narrow roads a few miles to the roundabout and then they were on the A1. It would take them a couple of hours to get to the house, but they were on their way.

After a while, they pulled up to eat.

"Do we really have time for this?" Gail asked.

Jesse knew she was in a hurry. Since she had believed in spirits and since she had been able to contact them, she had become hooked. Right now all she wanted to do was rush in and if he let her, she would. The problem was that could be dangerous.

"I know you're in a hurry, but Rosie was trapped in that house for days. Unable to escape, unable to contact anyone. If that happens to us, we need a few supplies with us, and we want a decent meal inside of us. Though it seems like a waste of time, it is worth it."

Gail nodded, and they entered the services. Quickly Jesse grabbed a few things from the shop. Crisps, chocolate, and drinks. They were all things that could be eating easily and would provide instant energy, even if they would also provide a sugar rush. It didn't matter, for what they were going into it would keep them going. Then they went to the restaurant and had a quick meal. This time they both chose something with plenty of protein. Within 20 minutes they were back on the road with Gail driving.

"I know you feel guilty about Rosie," Gail said.

Jesse nodded but said nothing. He didn't trust his voice. Of course, he felt guilty. They had freed her from the spirit but not in time. People had died, and she had ended up in a secure mental hospital probably for the rest of her life.

"It wasn't your fault," Gail said.

Jesse sighed. "I know, I just wish we could have stopped it sooner."

"We saved her life, we saved a lot of other lives. Suck it up and get over it."

Jesse laughed. "That actually helped."

"I know you."

Jesse nodded. She did, and she knew that flimsy condolences wouldn't help. At the end of the day what was done couldn't be changed, they had to look forward. There were new lives in danger, and he would fail if he were stuck in the past.

"I'm gonna see who I can contact, you okay to drive?"

"Yeah, you go ahead."

Jesse relaxed back and tried to contact his spirit guides. Something most people didn't know was that we all have them. They are there to help us in our time of need. Though some could be mischievous and others could even be dangerous. Jesse had three that he knew of, his grandmother Sylvia who had only just started communicating with him after years of ignoring him. An old man who used to haunt him as a child and who had helped on occasion. Jesse knew very little about him, and he still didn't trust the laughing ghost's motives. And then there was the dog he had as a child. A big brindle boxer full of love and loyalty to the end and beyond. Rose was the easiest of his spirit guides to contact. In the past she had helped him and saved Gail's life, however, it was hard to communicate with her and even she at times deserted him.

This time no one would contact him, not even the dog. It always worried him when this happened. Did it mean they thought he shouldn't go? Or, as Sylvia had once said to him, that he didn't need their help? She had also told him that if he relaxed and let go, he could be sensitive again. What she hadn't told him, was how to relax, and so far he hadn't mastered it.

The journey took longer than they expected and by the time they arrived at the house, it was well and truly dark. Gail pulled up alongside a blue Clio. Brambles and grass had grown all around the car. Some even snaked across the bonnet. It looked as if the vehicle had been dumped there months ago and yet they knew it was less than two days.

They got out of the vehicle, and Jesse pulled his phone from his pocket and tried calling Shelly once more. This time his phone wouldn't connect, he looked at it to see that there was no signal. Of course, there was no signal, this could never be easy.

"What should we take?" Gail asked as she came up beside him. "Meters, cameras, the EMF?"

Jesse smiled and walked to the back of the vehicle he grabbed an EMF meter, though he doubted they would need it, and put it in a small rucksack with the food. Then he grabbed an extra bottle of Holy Water and an additional torch and handed those to Gail.

"We don't need most of the stuff. We know there are spirits here, we know this is a hostile haunting. What we need is stuff to send these ghosts back, that's what I intend to do."

Moonlight gave them some visibility and they looked up at RedRise House. Jesse felt a shiver run down his back. It was a big house, impressive and looked in reasonable condition but he knew that was just a front. Rosie had told them how the property had decayed once Matron left it. That meant there were strong spirits in there. Spirits that wanted to stay there for if it were just the children, the lost souls, then they wouldn't spend their energy on creating this mirage. Dark windows stared back at them like angry eyes determined to keep them out. The place had a presence, even he could feel it, and it was not a nice one.

"What do you feel?" he asked.

Gail shivered and looked at the house with apprehension. "I can't connect to anything but there is a darkness here that I'm really not keen on."

"Way to underestimate." Jesse put a hand on her shoulder and squeezed gently. "Don't try to connect to anyone or anything. Do you have your protection?"

Gail showed him the necklace she was wearing. It was turquoise, imbued with white sage, orgonite and a silver tree of life. Very similar to the black bracelet he wore.

Each week, he blessed them both and dipped them in Holy Water to cleanse their aura. They helped protect them against being enraptured by a spirit. It was not infallible, but it was a help.

"Then we are ready." Gently he squeezed her shoulder one more time and ignored the feeling, the instinct that told him to run.

They walked along the overgrown path. The weeds and the brambles snagged at their feet hampering their progress as they struggled to the front door of the property. Once there he tried the door. He hadn't been sure what he expected, would the property welcome them, would it want more souls? Or would it have defenses to keep them out? His hand touched the handle, a slight shock went through him. It was just like static and yet it told him all he needed. They wouldn't be invited in.

Taking out his Holy Water he sprinkled some on the handle and began to recite the Lord's Prayer. Once that was done he tried again. It was no use the door was sealed tight.

"Should we shout out to them?" Gail asked.

"I don't think it will help. If they won't let us in, then they won't let them hear anything. There is one person who can help. I expected him to be here. To be waiting for us."

"Nick." Gail spun around and closed her eyes.

Jesse shook her shoulder. "Don't try and contact him... not that way, for you will let the others in."

"Then what do we do." The frustration was clear in her voice and the way that her fists were clenched in front of her. He could almost imagine her stamping her feet. It lifted the mood despite the danger.

"We call out to him in the normal way, we look for him. If we don't find him, then I'm sure I can get us in... it will just take longer."

Gail nodded opened her mouth and yelled, "Nick where are you?"

Jesse laughed and then they both shouted, called, and looked around the house but he was nowhere to be found.

"This is taking too long," Gail said.

Jesse couldn't deny she was right. His own stomach was filled with bile at the thought of the young Ghost Hunters inside that terrible house but what could he do? Then he remembered what Rosie had said. "Come on, I know where we can find him."

Without waiting for her to acknowledge him Jesse turned and ran along the overgrown path. The weeds snagged at his trousers and almost pulled him to the ground, but, he shook his legs free and kept going. Time was getting short. Like sand in an hour class, he could feel it trickling away, he only hoped it wasn't the life of Shelly and Jack emptying from that glass.

"Where are we going?" Gail asked.

"This way, it's just a little further."

Jesse was running through the woods his torch lighting up the path before them. Soon he came out into a clearing.

There amongst the long grass was an old and crumbling gravestone.

Stood behind it was Nick Aubrey.

"We need your help, Nick," Jesse said. "The house won't let us in."

Nick flickered and started to fade, Jesse wanted to shout and scream at him — don't you dare. Maybe he heard for he came back and moved closer to them.

"I thought I needed to see this through," Nick said his voice whispery and encased in static. "But I am so very tired. I won't go in that house, not again."

"We need your help," Jesse said biting down his frustration. "We need you to get us in that house and to help us end this once and for all."

Nick faded until they could see straight through him. Frustrated, Jesse searched through his memory for a ritual to bind him here but Gail put a hand on his shoulder.

"I feel your pain," she said. "You have suffered so much. I understand how hard this is for you. The guilt you have felt all down the years and the failure. So many times you have tried to prevent this, to stop Matron and that house from taking souls and so many times you have failed."

Nick looked up at her, they could still see the clearing through him. He nodded, and the look on his face broke Jesse's heart.

"We should let him go," Gail said, she was looking at Jesse.

He wanted to agree with her, to allow the tortured priest his peace, but he couldn't — not yet. Not when they needed him to save lives and then it came to him. "Maybe this is your chance for redemption. Maybe this is how you find your peace. All these years you have learned things that no one else could know. Use that knowledge and help us save this couple then I promise you that we will let you find your peace. We will help you find it."

Nick wavered in the air and blinked out of existence. There was nothing but the dark clearing lit by only the moon. A soft breeze lifted Gail's hair, he could see the tears in her eyes.

"Has he gone?" Jesse asked.

"No, he wants to go desperately. I think we should let him. I can feel his pain, his torment, it breaks my heart. The things he has had to watch. I don't think he is strong enough to watch it again."

Jesse sighed and paced over to the grave. He put his hand on the hard, cold stone and tried to open his mind. Maybe if he let go of his own guilt, then he would feel the spirit's vibration. Then he would understand and maybe he could use that to persuade Nick to help them. Only nothing came, no feeling, no insight, no nothing.

"Dammit, we don't have time for this." He walked back to Gail. "If you want to spend time with Nick then you are on your own. I have to get into that house... it's going to take some time. Let's just hope that Shelly and Jack have that time."

"If you could feel his pain you would understand," Gail said, but he could see in her eyes that she had her doubts. Thinking about the young couple's death was a stark reminder of the stakes they were playing.

"Maybe, but we need his help. Nick, damn you just get us into the house... if you can."

The words echoed in the air, the only sound in return was the rustling of the leaves and an owl hooted in the distance.

"He won't help, I have to go," Jesse said and turned to leave the clearing.

The sound of a scream echoed through the night, Jesse knew that their time had run out. They had to get into the house, and they had to do it now.

CHAPTER 14

*S*helly scraped her hands at the door so desperately, so hard that blood was soon covering the woodwork. In the dark, she couldn't see it, and in her panic, she couldn't feel it. All she knew was that something was behind her and it was getting closer. She had forgotten about Jack, forgotten the adventure this was supposed to be, the only thing in her mind was that death was stalking the darkness.

She had been trying to scream, but nothing would come, the only thing that escaped her were desperate, pitiful gasps. Now she was hyperventilating, and part of her knew that if she didn't stop soon that she would faint. Only how could she stop? Terror was a living beast creeping up behind her, if she didn't escape soon, it would consume her.

A touch on her shoulder, something hard, maybe the stick, finally released the scream and she wailed as loud as she could. She knew the sound would go nowhere, and even if it did there was no one to hear, but still, it broke the spell.

She turned to face her assailant but could see nothing. Her heart beat in her chest so hard she believed it must soon burst. Why couldn't she see? Even in the darkest night, you could always see something. After a few seconds, your eyes always adjusted. So why couldn't she see?

The sound of a stick scraped across the wooden floor was so close. Was it coming for her? Was that stick the way she died. Bashed over the head or stabbed through the heart?

"No, leave me alone," Shelly shouted into the darkness and all was still, all was silent.

The inky black consumed everything, even the air in the room, making it impossible to breathe, to think, and now to move. At last her knees gave way and she sank to the floor as she did her hand found her phone. The simple movement sent a flash of light into the room. Through it, she saw a young girl with long straggly hair and a bleak face. The girl was staring at her with hungry eyes. One finger was held up in the eternal signal for silence, in her other hand, she held the stick. It was a piece of two by two. Sturdy enough to be a weapon and up above her shoulders it filled Shelly's vision. She wanted to shrink from it but where could she go? How could she escape?

"Leave me alone," she sobbed into the darkness as the phone switched off.

Her desperate fingers sort out the button trying to switch it back on, to bring light back to the black. Only she couldn't do it, which was ridiculous, she knew that phone like the back of her hand. How could such a simple task escape her?

Once more the darkness seemed to stalk toward her. The scraping sound strummed her nerves like a virtuoso would tantalize his strings.

Scrape... scrape... scrape.

Where was the noise coming from? What was the point of it?

Then the sound stopped. Her head flicked this way and that, trying to hear, trying to discern if anything else hid within the devil's obscurity. There was nothing, not even a sigh, not a thing and that was worse for it gave her no idea where the girl was. If she was even still there.

Holding her breath, she imagined the stick above her. Ready to rush down and crush her skull. Fighting back her tears she tried to think, what could she do? There was nothing.

Then she heard another sound, it made her jump and scoot back toward the door until her back crashed against it. As she cowered in the darkness, she realized the sound was her own sobbing, for a moment she almost laughed. Not laughed with joy or even humor, she was close to hysteria, and part of her knew she had to hold on.

"What do you want?" She had wanted to shout the words but what came out was little more than a whimper.

There was no answer just the darkness.

"I came here to help you, tell me what you want."

The sound of a child's mocking laughter and the scrape of that stick to her left was the only reply she got, but the darkness lifted a little.

"That's it, let me help you. I can give you peace. I can let you leave this place... all you have to do is let me."

The darkness lifted a little more, she could see the girl in front of her. There was a sneer on her face, and the look in her eyes was enough to have Shelly pushing back against the door. The stick was in her left hand slicing through the air like a sword, and yet it made no breeze.

Then she heard a light and joyful laugh from the other side of the room. Turning she saw the young boy. The one who had helped her, the one she trusted.

"Hello," she said

He smiled in such a cute way that she wanted to go to him.

"Can you help me?"

He nodded, the light came on to reveal an empty room with peeling paintwork and stains on the walls and wooden floor. The boy was not quite corporeal and surrounded by a light mist. He was looking across to where the girl must be, Shelly found her eyes following his.

The girl was still there. She shook her head as if to say no. Now the stick was touching the floor and as Shelly watched she scraped it back and forth. Her scowl still pulled her face down, and she too was a little translucent only the mist that surrounded her was dark.

Did this mean it was too late for her? Could she not be saved?

Shelly didn't want to think about this, so she gave the girl a smile, and turned back to the boy.

"Can you get me out of here?" she asked.

The question widened his eyes. The smile slipped off his face. Gently he shook his head and looked at the girl.

Shelly wished she knew what she was doing. If she had brought some salt or remembered the rituals, then she would have a chance. All she expected from the house was to have a session with the Ouija board and have a few conversations with spirits. Then she had intended to get one of them to communicate with her sister. To apologize and then she expected to say a few words and leave.

How had it all gone so wrong?

Because you know nothing. The words were inside her head.

Part of her wanted to argue, but the girl was right.

"I meant no harm, just to help you... I just wanted to see, to hear, and to tell her I was sorry.

She knows the voice was a young child's voice, the boys. Shelly turned to him and smiled her gratitude.

In one moment he was stood across the room and then he flickered and in the next, he was stood in front of her his hand held out before him.

Shelly gasped, but she knew he wanted to help, and now she believed that he would.

She reached out to take his hand... her fingers went straight through his. There was nothing but a touch of cold and a feeling of static.

He shrugged and leaned his head to the left.

Shelly nodded and climbed to her feet.

The door opened, and she walked out into the hallway.

"Can you help me find Jack?" she asked looking behind her, but the boy had gone.

Yes, the voice was in her head. She whipped around to see him in the corridor walking toward the stairs. *But it may be too late.*

127

*J*esse left the dark clearing and raced back through the woodland. Branches whipped at his face and brambles snagged at his feet, but he wouldn't slow down. The torchlight flashed at he ran causing shadows. Places for him to trip and almost fall, but it was enough for him to find his way as he rushed down the dark path as quickly as he could.

Part of him knew he had to get into that house and he had to do it now. It wasn't just the scream, it wasn't because he was *sensitive*, after all, he *wasn't* anymore, but something told him it had to be now. It was like he had a connection and yet he couldn't explain it. Maybe it was guilt, just guilt because he should have neutralized this house some time ago. There was also anger. A deep fury at the ghostly priest because he refused to help them. What did he have to lose? The man had been dead for years. They had already offered to send him to peace. All he needed to do was to be brave for just one more time. To help them gain entry, was that too much to ask? Jesse didn't think it was and he was angry and disappointed at himself because he didn't have the skills to persuade the spirit to help.

He could hear that Gail was behind him, but he rushed on hoping to get into the house before she arrived with him. She was anxious and confident. If he wasn't careful she would use her power, her sensitivity, and she would contact whatever was in there. Her ability was strong, she believed she could handle anything she met, only Jesse had a bad feeling about this and his instincts, his gut, told him it was better if she didn't connect until they knew more.

Part of him had hoped she would stay in the clearing. That with her empathy and people skills she would be able to persuade Nick to join them. To help them this one last time before he was sent to peace. He wasn't sure why she had followed him because he knew how much she cared. In her mind she was ready to set Nick free, she would believe it was his right, he just hoped she wouldn't have done it just yet. He hoped that once she had spoken to him, connected with him a little more, she would have understood that he needed to do this as much as they needed him. Only there had been no time to explain all of this. Now he was racing through the darkness, through the trees, toward God only knows what.

Panting heavily Jesse ran out onto the gravel and passed the two cars. Without pausing, he jumped over the undergrowth and trampled more of it as he made his way along the overgrown path up to the house.

His bag was still at the door with the equipment and Holy Water waiting for him. Placing his hand on the door, he recited the releasing prayer. All his intention asked the higher power to release the door. Then he sprinkled the handle with Holy Water closed his eyes and turned the handle.

Nothing happened.

Gail arrived at his side panting, red-faced, she raised her eyebrows to ask.

He shook his head, they were getting nowhere at least not yet.

Though he had been stood still now for several minutes, he was still gasping for breath. The effort of putting all of his intentions into opening the door was just as hard as racing through the woods. Concentrating he built up his power inside, built up all the intention and all the energy he had. Directing that thought through his right hand on the handle, he sprinkled Holy Water on the door with his left hand.

"I command you open by the power of Jesus Christ. Release all ungodly hold on this gateway and let us pass."

Sweat was running down his neck, and the muscles in his shoulders shook with the effort. Relaxing just a moment he tried to turn the handle.

It could have been set in stone because there was no way that he could move it.

"Aaarrgghh," he yelled out his frustration into the night.

"It's okay." Gail put her hand on his shoulder and tensed muscles. "Let me try. There will be good spirits in there, I can contact them, I can get us inside."

"No!" Jesse snapped the words much more harshly than he intended.

"Dammit Jesse, then why am I here if you won't let me help?"

"Look I... It's not that I don't want you to help, it's not that I don't believe in you... in all the power that you have... it's just a feeling... I can't explain it more than that. It's not fear for you or foolish male protection... something... I guess you would say my gut is telling me you shouldn't do this."

"Yes but maybe I should, maybe I'm strong enough. I can do this."

Jesse could see the strength and beauty of her. He loved her so much that it hurt to tell her no. But every instinct he had, said that he must.

"I hear you Gail I really do but trust my experience. A lot of what we do is done on a feeling. I may not be sensitive anymore, but Sylvia told me to trust myself, in this incident I do."

Gail nodded. "I understand. I will listen to you for at least a little longer. She also told you to reach for your power. Maybe you should try that one too?"

Jesse nodded and wondered if it was worth a try.

Gail was looking at him, her arms crossed, her eyebrows raised, so he guessed he had no choice. The problem was he didn't really know what Sylvia meant.

He shrugged and closed his eyes. Letting out a sigh he then took in three deep breaths and tried to enter a meditative state. It was difficult. All his mind wanted to do was work the problem. How did they get in? What else could he do? Could he still get Nick here? Should he let Gail try? How did they get in? Around and around his monkey brain wanted to go but he reigned it in and tied it down and forced himself to think of nothing. It was so hard when time was so desperately short, but he was getting better at this. Soon he was relaxed enough to call out for his spirit guides.

"Guide me wise ones. Be with me in the dark places and

guide me back to the light. I call on you my spirit guides to help me out tonight. Help me enter this place of darkness to bring those inside back to the light."

With his eyes still closed he let his mind feel out into the veil hoping for any sign any touch from his guides.

The contact was almost instant, and he couldn't stop the smile from spreading across his face. He was enveloped in a feeling of warmth and love. Suddenly his face was warm and wet as if the moist tongue of his favorite boxer dog had just given him a great big kiss. Looking down to his feet he saw Rose sat there. There was a twinkle in her eye, and he could swear there was a smile on her face. She whined gently and then turned to look at the woods. Taking a few steps, she looked back and whined at him again.

Jesse nodded at her and then shook his head. He understood Rose wanted him to go back to Nick's grave... it was too far. It would take 10 minutes to get back there another 10 minutes to get back here, by that time, the young couple could already be dead.

"Rose it's so wonderful to see you but help me get in here, I haven't got the time to find the priest."

Rose walked a few steps further away looked back and whined again, then she woofed at him a little frustrated, trotted back, and then trotted away again.

"I haven't got time maybe Gail can go with you?"

Rose came back to him and laid down at his side letting out a mournful moan that tore out his heart and brought tears to his eyes.

"I'm so sorry Rose... I don't have time."

The sound of an old man's laughter echoed from the edge of the woods. Jesse looked up.

Peeking out from behind a large oak tree was an old man dressed in dark clothes his white hair stood up on his head like he had just got out of bed. There was an inane grin on his face, and he was pointing into the trees. Jesse recognized him immediately. It was the laughing man, the second of his spirit guides, the one he couldn't make out. The one who had haunted him as a child and scared the crap out of him on more times than he could count. So even the laughing man wanted him to go find Nick, but there wasn't time. He was about to open his eyes to tell Gail to go with the other two spirits when an old and gentle woman's voice spoke in his mind.

My sweet boy trust us to guide you back to the light. The priest is what you need, but you do not need to run to find him. Reach for your power, and you will find it there. Believe in yourself, connect with Nick. Understand his suffering and show him yours and you will find your way.

"Sylvia, Sylvia it is so good to hear your voice. I don't understand. I don't have any power."

You have all the power that you need, the voice was fading as if it was blown away by the wind. *Trust me, my sweet boy, for there is very little time left.*

CHAPTER 16

*S*helly followed the little boy down the stairs. The tatty trousers around his feet and ankles and his elbows stuck out painfully from the smock. Occasionally, he would look back. There was always a cheeky smile on his gaunt face. Despite her desperation and the need to hurry, she had the urge to hug him. To pull him into her arms and to tell him that everything would be okay. But she knew that was useless. He was a spirit. Her arms would go straight through him.

As he walked down the stairs, the light began to dim. It was imperceptible at first. Though she knew something was wrong, she couldn't figure out what it was, so she kept looking around trying to work out what had changed. Breathing was harder. Was that because she was excited, anxious, or was it really happening? The further she descended, the darker it became. Fear was the monkey on her back. Shouting at her to run, run, run.

It was what she wanted to do. To race down the stairs screaming for Jack. Bursting into every room until she found him. But she knew that wouldn't work. The house too big and something was hiding him from her. Some of the children were good, some of them were not; it was her job to work out which was which.

"Do you know where Jack is?"

The boy turned around and nodded, but his eyes were wide and moist with unshed tears.

"Are you taking me to him?"

His mouth opened and closed, but no sound came out.

Shelly knew he could communicate within her mind, he had done it before. So why wasn't he doing it now? Did he have something to hide?

They got to the bottom of the stairs, and her only light was the torch. It cast shadows across the walls and left so many hiding places. The darkness loomed toward her, and she was constantly turning her head searching, but searching for what?

In front of her, across the huge hall, was the front door. For a moment she wanted to run to it. To yank it open and to escape from this dreadful place, but she couldn't do it. She couldn't leave Jack, and even if she made such a cowardly move, would the house let her escape? Somehow, she doubted it.

The little boy hesitated as he reached the center of the room. His eyes scanned the room and then were pulled back to the kitchen. Again, he tried to look away, to turn toward the library. But those sad, moist eyes were snapping back like a yo-yo hitting the end of its string.

The dim light and the brightness of the torch gave him a

skeletal effect. It sunk his eyes into his cheeks and created shadows around his face. Unlike his fear, it was just an illusion. He looked down toward the corridor, and then back at the kitchen. His eyes hardly rested on the kitchen doorway before he looked elsewhere. This time it was the library. And then he looked at her, but he couldn't manage a smile.

"Do we need to go to the kitchen?" she asked him.

For a moment he turned away from her and started to fade. Would he disappear? Would he leave her once more, unable to find Jack and all alone?

"Don't leave me."

He nodded and turned to look at her. His eyes screwed tightly and full of tears, his jaw was clenched as if he were trying to prevent it from betraying him.

Shelly finally understood. "Where you're taking me… you're frightened. You think it's dangerous, and you're worried that I will be… that I will be trapped?"

He nodded and lowered his eyes to the ground, refusing to lift them again.

Shelly dropped to her knees beside him, and with her hand, she tried to lift his chin. Her fingers felt nothing but cold moisture and a slight electric charge. For a moment the boy wavered, stepped back, but then he was there again. With a shrug of his shoulders, he apologized.

I know where Jack is, the words were inside her head. The voice wavered, and she could hear the sound of him swallowing. *Don't follow me, don't go to him or they will have you, too.*

Shelly nodded.

You made a promise... keep it.

Warm tears flooded into Shelly's eyes, she swallowed hard to fight the lump in her throat. "I have to find him, no matter what."

Then you won't send me to the good place... you won't be able to.

"I will, I promise... or you could just she tell me where he is and I will..." She couldn't remember the words, couldn't even remember the wording of the releasing ritual she had promised she would use. "We can go back to the room, and I could release you now."

For a moment he stepped from foot to foot like a young child desperate for the bathroom.

Despite the terrible situation, it brought a smile to Shelly's face. His childhood had been a living hell. He was still in a living hell, and had been for possibly centuries, and yet he was still a young child. She had to let him go, and as she had that thought, the majority of the releasing ritual came back to her, and she understood. If she said it with intention, then he would be freed.

"I can do it. I can let you go. Just tell me where Jack is?"

He looked up at her, his eyes bright. Tears had cleaned two tracks down his dirty face, and his rosie lips quivered. *I can't. They won't let me. They will hurt me.*

"I won't let them."

At this, the little boy shrugged his shoulders and Shelly understood. He knew she had no power. He knew that she was powerless to help herself, let alone him or Jack.

Once more she looked at the door and the possibility of escape. It was so close and so tempting. No, she wouldn't be beaten. She came here to pass a message to the sister she had lost. The one who helped her escape a burning vehicle. The one she couldn't save. The one who helped her after she was dead. All she had wanted to do for the past six years was to tell her sister she was sorry — that was why she was here. It had been foolish and selfish, and it had gotten her best friend killed. However, she would follow this boy to wherever he lead. She would find Jack, even if it meant she would join him.

"I understand we are heading into danger, but would you take me to him?"

The little boy nodded. He shimmered out of existence and then back in a few feet away. Then he walked slowly toward the kitchen. The closer he got to it, the more translucent he became. She was losing him.

Shelly rushed to the kitchen to see him disappearing into a wall... and he was gone.

Racing to the wall, she ran her hands over the surface. There was nothing, nothing to let her in. So, she knocked on the wall from top to bottom, left to right trying to find an area that was hollow, trying to find an area with a knocking sound that was different, but there was nothing.

At her left was the door, the one with the notice on it telling them to keep out. That had to be where he had gone, and yet looking at the door filled her with dread. It would lead down into a cellar, it would be darker than this room. It would be a dungeon of terrors and fear, and she doubted she would escape it alive.

It didn't matter. She had to go, so she walked over to the door and grasped onto the handle. It was cold. A slight shock tingled her fingers as she touched it but try as she might, she couldn't turn it. Pulling, pushing, and wrenching at the door did nothing. Frustrated, she kicked the wood. Shock raced through her toes like she had kicked solid concrete. Pulling back, she let out a cry of frustration and pain and sank to the floor. Tears of despair and defeat enveloped her.

She had failed her sister. She had failed Jack, and now she couldn't escape this house and would soon become its next sacrifice. Then a thought crossed her mind. She could stop anyone else from suffering. She could burn it to the ground.

For a few moments more she let the tears come, let them wash away her despair. As she cried, she didn't notice that it was getting lighter and then she felt a hand on her shoulder. As she looked up, she felt her heart break.

CHAPTER 17

"*R*elax and seek out the godly one!" Jesse paced toward the overgrown garden and then back to the house. "Dammit, Sylvia, what do you mean, seek out the godly one? I don't understand you. Why won't you help me?" His hands were raised in the air beseeching the spirit to come back. To explain. To do anything that would make this easier for him. Once again, all he had gotten was riddles and questions but never any answers.

"She means the priest," Gail said.

Jesse couldn't hear her. He was locked in his own mind trying to fathom out a solution to the problem, and he let out a yelp as Gail touched his shoulder.

"Hey, it's just me," she said, and smiled as he grimaced at his own twitchiness. "The godly one? Sylvia I presume?" She raised her eyebrows.

Jesse nodded.

"She's talking about the priest. Relax... I'm pretty sure she told you to relax and try to connect with him like I connect to the spirits."

Jesse clenched his fists in front of his face trying to express the frustration. It was no good. "I understand that, but I don't understand why she thinks I can. We both know I lost my gift... I can't communicate with spirits. That's why you're here. When she told me to use my power, I thought she meant you... yet every nerve in my body is telling me not to let you try this."

Gail walked up to him and took his hands, lowering them down and holding them tightly. "I know, and I know how hard you tried to reconnect with your gift. Maybe this is different. Maybe Sylvia knows something, and maybe, just maybe you should trust her."

"That's a lot of maybes." Jesse smiled and took strength from her touch. "I guess I've got nothing to lose. I tried every trick I know and we're not getting in there. The spirits are too strong, too many."

"Then let's do this. Let's see if you can connect to Nick, and let's see if that's the answer."

For a moment, he pulled her into his arms and gained strength from the support and love she offered so freely. All the years they had been together, Gail had never believed, and yet she had never doubted his belief. She had never chastised him for believing or for the search that he made. She was his rock, his heart, and his soul. She had been perfect for him, even when she didn't believe. But then last year, when she finally saw a ghost, and was finally converted to a believer, she became just the most amazing person ever.

Still, he didn't know what to do. When he had seen spirits as a child, it had taken no effort. They were just there. At first, it was very scary, but then, as he got to understood them, the excitement, the buzz of seeing them became like a drug.

Then after the death of his grandfather, he lost his talent. Once before Sylvia had told him that it was guilt holding him back. He didn't believe that. Yes, he had been the cause of his grandfather's death in a very roundabout way, but he understood, he had been just a child — it wasn't his fault. So why would that cause him to lose his talent?

Gail squeezed his fingers. "Hey, you can do this. I'm here if you need me."

Jesse nodded. She was right, this was not the time to be worrying about the past. The present was all that mattered. Saving the young Ghost Hunters was why he was here. He would try anything, even if he didn't think it would work, to make that happen.

"Okay, I'm ready."

He squeezed her fingers once more and then pulled his hands free, shaking them out before him and jogging on the spot for just a moment. He looked a little bit like a runner limbering up for a race, but the idea was to free his muscles and to release tension. The movement would help relax his mind, as well as his body. When he felt as if he was as relaxed as he was going to get, he stopped and closed his eyes.

With them closed, he took in a long slow breath counting to six as he breathed in. He let it out to the count of seven and then breathed in to the count of seven. Holding it for a full three seconds, he let it out to the count of eight and then breathed in to the count of eight. This time he held it for four seconds and then as he let it out, he let his whole body and mind relax and he searched for Nick's mind.

At first, there was nothing just darkness and that feeling that he should be doing something. The monkey brain was nagging, trying to regain control. He shut it down quickly and thought of nothing but Nick. He imagined the priest in his head, his brown hair, the old-fashioned suit, the dog collar. Soon he had a picture of him standing in the small clearing next to the crumbling gravestone. Nick was looking away, his shoulders slumped, his body a picture of defeat.

Jesse didn't know whether this was working or whether it was just his imagination, but he pushed his mind out and tried to communicate with Nick.

The priest jumped and turned around. The look on his face was of annoyance and fear, but he hid it quickly and replaced it with the calm, stoic exterior that Jesse was used to seeing.

"I need your help," Jessie said.

Nick shook his head and started to fade. Soon he was nothing but an imprint, a faint shadow against the blackness of the trees.

"Then explain it to me," Jesse said. "If you won't help me, then have the decency to explain to me why you would let those two die."

As well as talking, he was projecting his mind toward the priest. It was a strange sensation and something he didn't totally understand. But as he did it, he was no longer standing next to the house - he was there in the clearing and standing next to Nick. Something told him to reach out and touch the spirit. His logical mind laughed at the idea. Nick was incorporeal, he couldn't touch him. Still, his projected body reacted and reached out, grabbing hold of the priest's arm.

Jesse was as shocked as Nick when he took hold of his arm and held him there.

"I... I don't believe this."

Nick's eyes were wide, Jesse knew that he didn't either. There was no time for wonder they had to move quickly.

"Explain to me, show me why you won't help." Jesse didn't know why he had said that. The words just came into his mind and were out before he could even think of a reason.

Nick threw back his head. His skin melted away leaving nothing but a skull. The jaw opening in a scream of eternal anguish.

Jesse was flooded with feelings of fear, anger, terror, disgust, and more. It was so strong, it dropped him to his knees and then he was no longer there. For a moment, he thought he had lost the connection that he was back in his own body, back at RedRise House. But as he looked out, he realized he was connected to the priest in a much deeper way. They were joined. He was inside the man's head and seeing through his eyes. At first, he was just looking at the clearing, at the grave, and he felt intense sadness, but more than that, there was despair and guilt. He knew people had died because he hadn't saved them, and it was eating him up inside.

Everything flashed, then he was inside RedRise House. Though he had never been to the room, he recognized it from Rosie's account. It was *the* room, the cavernous room carved out of the ground that was hidden somewhere beneath the house.

It was cold and he could hear the sound of running water, but above that, he could hear the sound of chanting in Latin.

It was a sacrificial ritual. He recognized the odd words, but his mind wouldn't concentrate on what they were singing.

He was pulled across the room toward a corner where a group of children and five adults was surrounded by four flickering torches. Fear weakened his knees and clenched tightly onto his heart. Fear was like an army drummer pounding in his chest as he walked closer and closer, until he could see over the backs of the children.

They were surrounding a stone sacrificial altar. Held onto it by four cloaked adults was a young girl. She was dirty and thin and wearing a ragged dress. The fight had gone out of her. At one stage, the adults had pinned her to that bench, holding each of her limbs so she couldn't escape. They didn't need to now… she was frozen in her own mortality.

Jesse watched as the fifth adult who was smaller than the others, pulled a wicked curved knife from within her robe. He knew this would be Matron, the Old Hag, the spirit they had sent away.

Jesse felt the pain slice through Nick's stomach as he had to watch that blade arch into the air and come hurtling down to rip out the throat of the young girl. Jesse watched as he tried and failed to stop the sacrifice.

"I understand," he said. "I know you had to witness awful things, but if you don't help me, it will happen again."

Images flashed before Jesse's mind. Like a torture film on fast forward, he watched a girl killed, a boy killed, another boy. Nick tried to stop it, but he wasn't there. Was just a spirit. No matter how much he shouted, tried to fight, it made no difference. He couldn't interact, couldn't do anything but watch.

One after the other they flashed up. Over and again he watched the horrific image of a child's life ripped from its body. And each time it happened, the child joined the ranks of those tormented creatures stood around the altar. Nick felt their every emotion: their fear, despair, and eventually, their acceptance as they knew it was inevitable. That was the worst emotion. With that bitter taste in his mouth, he felt the pain as their throats were slashed. Their gasps for breath as the blood poured onto the stone. Their screams echoed through the night, and still, it wouldn't stop. Again, and again, and again he endured until he couldn't endure anymore, and suddenly he understood. Nick had borne it all, and he had been unable to stop any of it. He feared that he was a witness. Feared that they needed him for it to happen.

Jesse closed his eyes. The images flashed through his mind. He dropped to his knees and retched onto the floor, and still it wouldn't stop. This was not a recording, it was real. He could smell the blood, hear the screams, and feel the fluids splash across his skin. It was like a never-ending loop, and he knew that if he didn't get out of it soon, he would go insane. Was that what had happened to Nick? Maybe that was why he was here.

Once more, he closed his eyes and took a deep breath, counting in one, two, three, four, five, six. The images were still there, but he forced them out of his mind, forced himself to concentrate on nothing but the counting. He breathed out for seven. Breathing in for seven, he managed to stop some of the images, managed to take back a little bit of control. Concentrating on the numbers one, two, three, four, five, six, seven, eight, he breathed out.

The altar and the figures had faded into the distance, and he breathed in to the count of eight. As he breathed out to the count of nine, he felt the breeze in his hair, and as he opened his eyes, he was back in front of the house, his hand clasped onto Nick's arm.

He heard Gail gasp and knew that she had seen him. There was no time to talk to her, to explain. He had to do this now — before he lost Nick again.

"I understand how you feel, but you are wrong. You are not the witness; you are the key. You can help me, you can save these two young people and when you do, you will finally rest in peace."

For long moments Nick didn't move. The slight breeze ruffled his brown hair but his eyes looked empty. Jesse began to wonder if he had heard him. Then, at last, he looked up. There was hope in his eyes, and he nodded.

$\mathcal{S}$helly looked up into brown eyes and hair that were a match to her own. The face was younger, the nose not quite so prominent, the lips a little fuller. Her heart was pounding so fast she felt that it would explode in her chest, and hot tears streamed down her face. Her mouth opened and closed, but the lump in her throat wouldn't let the words pass.

Stacey, her sister, was finally here. She finally had the chance to make it right.

It's all right, said the voice in her head, one she recognized. *It's all right my beautiful Shelly, my wonderful twin. I know what you want to say. I have felt it from the minute you thought it. As I have also felt the torment you feel. I want it to stop. I want you to be happy and to let go of the needless guilt.*

Shelly reached out to grab her hands but her fingers went straight through. Her sister faded away just a little.

"No, don't leave me. There is so much I have to say."

You don't have to say anything... I have heard it a hundred times, and you owe me no apology. It was not your fault I died. Yes, you had to persuade me to go to that party, but that was normal, and as normal, I loved it once I got there." Stacey shrugged and raised her eyebrows. *"It wasn't your fault that John had been drinking. It wasn't your fault he lost control. And it wasn't your fault that you were the only one that survived.*

Love and guilt swarmed around Shelly's heart like bees around a honeypot. They never stopped, never settled, never gave her time to concentrate on just one of them, and the emotions were overwhelming. There was so much she wanted to say, but she didn't have time.

"I... I want to tell you so many things but..."

I know, Jack is in danger. I can take you to him, but I don't want to.

"Why?"

Because I think it is too late. You have talent. I couldn't have helped you that day if you didn't. Your agony at my loss called me back. I didn't save you... you saved me.

"That's not true. I never would have got out of the car without you. I would have burnt to death if you hadn't opened the door."

I didn't open the door. I'm a ghost, remember. You have tremendous talent. You moved that door, the problem is you don't know how to use that talent... not yet. If I take you to Jack... you may both die. Don't make me do that.

"We *may* die... but that means we *may* both live, and I have to take that chance. Please show me where he is."

A tear ran down Stacey's face, but she nodded her head. *I will do this, and I will help if I can. But you must understand, if you die here, I think you will stay here forever. I think this place is hell.*

Shelly gulped down her fear and swallowed the words that wanted to say *get me out of here*. She knew she could do this, knew she had to save Jack, and if she didn't, then it was only right that she died with him.

As she had the thoughts, she could see that Stacey heard them and she shook her head to apologize. "Lead the way, my twin. Together we ride against the forces of evil."

Onward to battle, Stacey answered.

These had been the words they used when they were children while fighting dragons and evil to save the handsome Prince. Who would, then, of course, marry them. They had been fun times, harmless fantasies of two girls growing up with endless imaginations. They gave her strength and faith. They had never been beaten in battle as children, and they were not going to lose now.

Stacey walked toward the door with the notice on it. It didn't surprise Shelly. A part of her knew that Jack had to be in the cellar, the dungeon. But would her sister have a way of getting through that locked door?

Stacey turned and nodded as if she had heard the question. She gave a smile that reminded Shelly of lazy sunny afternoons lying on a river bank and dreaming of love. Keeping this thought in her mind, she followed her sister. That one smile had washed away the guilt, washed away the fear. They were the unbeaten twins and once more they would battle evil.

Stacey disappeared, fading gradually into the door. The air buzzed slightly, and Shelly could see a mist surrounding the door. It was light and gave her a feeling of warmth and hope. As it faded, she heard the door click open. It looked like she was in.

Shelly pulled the door wide and peered down dark, narrow steps. They looked like they were carved out of stone and she could only see a few feet beyond the door. Waiting at the edge of her vision was Stacey.

Are you sure?

"I am."

Stacey nodded, turned, and floated down the stairwell. She took a little bit of light with her and Shelly hardly needed her torch to follow as long as she kept up. The sound of her feet slap, slap, slapping on the stone steps filled the tunnel and echoed back all around her. As she got to the 10th step, the door closed behind her with a slam, and she jumped so much that she almost toppled down into the darkness.

Don't worry, I can open it again, Stacey said in her mind.

"Good to know."

The further they walked the more disorienting it became. Down they went into darkness, into an underground cavern. It reminded her of a program she had once seen on potholing. All she could remember of it were the warnings, the dangers, and the one mantra – never go alone.

The walls swarmed toward her, her breathe coming hard and fast. Claustrophobia pushed on her chest like an amateur giving CPR. And with each pound of its fist, her heart jolted in and out of life. She knew she was panicking, hyperventilating, and that if she didn't get hold of herself, she would possibly faint.

Suddenly she was surrounded by light and by a feeling of love, and she looked up to see Stacey floating in front of her. Her sister was so beautiful and so full of love it took away much of the fear.

I am with you, Stacey said. *I will be with you until the end of this, and then we will talk. I hope we will talk a lot in the future, for I am staying close to you and going nowhere without you.*

Stacey let out a sob as tears of joy ran down her face.

"You were always the best sister. I have missed you so much."

Me too. Come on, not much further. Stacey turned and started to flow down the stairs once more.

Shelly followed her. As they hit bottom, she heard the sound of running water and the air was moist and stale. The stench of something long dead and rotten filled her nostrils and clawed at her throat. This place was death and every fiber of her wanted to flee from it.

This way, Stacey said, and turned to the left.

They ventured down a narrow passageway and passed a small alcove filled with books. Ahead of them was the door, and Shelly knew that behind it was a sacrificial chamber where she would find Jack.

Would they be in time?

Would he be alive?

In front of them was a heavy and rough wooden door. It was made out of planks with metal strips across it. Despite its age, it looked impenetrable, and for a moment Stacey faltered.

Turning, she looked at Shelly with tears in her eyes. *This is your last chance to turn around, to return to safety.*

Shelly bit down the reply that wanted to say, *get me out of here.*

"Is Jack alive?"

For a moment Stacey was gone and when she returned, she nodded. *The ritual is nearing its climax... there is still a chance.*

"Do not ask me to leave again, just help me."

The door is open. Stacey passed through it.

Just for a second, Shelly hesitated. She took a deep breath and imagined Jack's smile. The way he was always there for her. Then she put her hand on the door handle and pulled. It creaked as it opened and orange light flickered out into the passageway. Before her nerve could defeat her, she walked into a large chamber that appeared to be hewn out of solid rock. The light was coming from the far side of the room, and Stacey beckoned her forward.

Across the room, four flame torches were held high and surrounding what looked like a group of children and three adults. They all had their backs to her and had formed a semicircle, a U, around what she knew would be Jack.

Listen to your instincts, Stacey said as she floated toward the figures.

Shelly tried, but all she could feel was fear.

From across the room came a scream of abject terror

Before she knew what was happening, she was running across the room, and shouting, "Get away from him! Don't you hurt him! Get away from him, you bastards!"

The figures turned and parted as one. The children's faces were feral masks of hatred. The look in their eyes was enough to turn her blood to ice and their mouths... the teeth in them were ready to rip her apart if she stood in their way.

All dressed in black, they reminded her of rats on a film she had seen about the Pied Piper. Rats that would destroy everything in front of them — but could be beaten by one man. Why had that come to her mind? Was that her instincts? She didn't know. But she didn't know what else to do. So, she ran toward them.

"Get away from him, or I will send you back to hell!"

Then she remembered the releasing ritual that Rosie had told them about and how it would send the spirits back one by one. Could she use it to send all of them back in one go? She didn't know, but she was going to try.

Rosie had told her the most important thing was to fill any ritual, any exorcism, with the intention of rebuking the spirit. So, she gathered her anger, her fear, and her disgust at what these creatures had done and she piled it into her voice as she recited the prayer.

"In the Name of Jesus, I rebuke the spirits of RedRise House. I command you leave this place, without manifestation and without harm to me or anyone, so that He can dispose of you according to His Holy Will."

One of the children turned. Shelly stepped back. A gaunt face, black eyes so terrible that they bored into her, and the smile. The look on its face was one that she would remember for life. It would fill her nightmares. The child wanted to destroy her.

Standing, shaking, she wanted to run, but her legs wouldn't obey. So, she repeated the ritual, projecting it with all her being.

"In the Name of Jesus, I rebuke the spirits of RedRise House. I command you leave this place, without manifestation and without harm to me or anyone, so that He can dispose of you according to His Holy Will."

The mask of loathing dropped away, and in its place was a sweet smile on a dirty and emancipated face. He nodded at her and then faded, the black of his clothes turning lighter until he was like an angel who blinked out in the darkness.

Shelly was filled with delight, hope, and a feeling of glory. Another of the children approached her, a little girl this time. She nodded and mouthed the words, *thank you* and then she changed from a solid being of darkness into a mist of light before she, too was gone.

It was working. They were leaving, going to peace. If she had known it would have been this simple, she could have done this right at the beginning. It felt like weeks since they had entered the house, though it was probably less than 24 hours, but the exhaustion this had caused was more than she had ever felt. Now all she needed was for the other spirits to go so that she could get to Jack and then they could rest.

As if in answer to her thought, the children threw back their heads and she saw the gashes at the necks.

"No!" the word was torn from her as their life must have been torn from them. It was too horrible, too much to bear.

The hooded figure to her right threw back his hood. She recognized the man who had greeted them, Mr. Duncan.

155

He smiled at her recognition and pulled a wicked knife from his cloak. It was curved and glinted in the darkness. Flickering with the orange light as if it were alive, on fire, a blade of hell itself.

Stacey floated in between Shelly and the man but he flashed the knife through her — she dissipated and was gone.

"No!" Shelly screamed, her knees giving way. She dropped to the floor. It was over.

"Shelly, get out of here. Run!" Jack shouted.

She watched as he tried to get up off the altar, but was pushed back down before he could.

The other two hooded figures held onto his ankles and kept him there, pinning him down and holding him.

"In the Name of Jesus, I rebuke the spirits of RedRise House. I command you leave this place, without manifestation and without harm to me or anyone, so that He can dispose of you according to His Holy Will," Shelly shouted the words, and as she did so she advanced on the spirits. For a moment nothing happened and then all of the spirits faded away, but this was different somehow. They didn't change, didn't come to her, they just faded... then they were gone. Maybe that was because there were so many of them. It didn't matter, they were gone.

They haven't gone, they heard the others coming. Stacey said, as she appeared again, only this time she was much fainter, translucent, and her smile was missing. She moved over to the altar and looked down at Jack.

"The others!" Shelly asked as she followed her, but as she saw Jack she forgot about everything but him.

He was lying on the hard stone, his shirt off, his face bruised and bleeding as was his shoulder, but he was alive. Shelly reached out to touch him and his eyes opened, and he smiled up at her.

Shelly pulled him into her arms.

"I'm so glad you survived," she whispered into his ear. "I could have sworn I'd lost you and I don't think I could live without you. Jack, I should have told you this a while ago... I love you."

Jack held at arm's length, she could see him trying to speak. At first, the words wouldn't come, he just made a croaky scratchy sound. He swallowed, causing his Adam's apple to bounce in his throat. "I love you too. I have wanted to tell you for so long... I just... I never thought you would think of me as anything but a friend."

"You will always be my friend, but I want to be so much more."

Jack lifted her chin and found her lips with his. He tasted of blood and salt, but it was still the sweetest kiss she had ever had.

I don't mean to be a killjoy, but maybe we should get out of here, Stacey said in both of their minds.

They pulled apart. Jack stared over Shelly's shoulder.

"Can you see her," Shelly asked.

"Your dead sister? Yeah, she's right behind you. I always believed you, but I always had some doubt. I think that's gone now."

Jack laughed. "Can you stand?"

157

"Yeah, I think so."

Shelly helped him to his feet and let him lean upon her shoulder. "Then let's get out of here before they come back."

CHAPTER 19

"Can you help us get in," Jesse asked.

Beneath the hope, there was still fear in Nick's eyes, but he nodded his head and pointed to the side of the house.

"Follow me. There is an old service entrance on the far side of the house. Most of the owners forgot about its existence. The people who used it were not important to them, so they didn't see it."

"Can it be that simple?" Jesse asked. "They simply forgot it?"

Nick smiled and raised his eyebrows. It made him look so much younger and more relaxed. "I used to bless it every week and have still done so on occasion. The spirits avoid me as much as they can…"

"What?" Jesse knew there was more.

"I was always drawn to them when they made a sacrifice. It was as if I couldn't stay away. It is why I think I must be a witness."

Jesse thought about it and wondered if he was wrong, but he didn't think so. "Why would you have to be there?" Though he said the words aloud, they were really said to himself, to what Sylvia probably thought of as his power. When he spoke like this, he often received insights and now was no different. He understood.

"You have tied yourself to them. Your guilt at not stopping this has linked your destiny with theirs. You are not a witness. In fact, you could be our secret weapon. Come on, we must hurry."

Nick nodded and walked easily through the overgrown garden. It was not so easy for Gail and Jesse. Luckily it was getting lighter by the minute. Even so, they had to struggle over brambles, weeds, and even sapling trees that had rooted there. Everything was wild and distorted, and as he pushed through, it reminded Jesse of a post-apocalyptic world. Something he had only read about.

"Ouch."

Jesse turned to see Gail on her knees, he rushed back to her.

"Are you all right?" He helped her up to find thick rose tendrils with vicious thorns had wrapped around her legs. There was a speck of blood on her cheek and more soaking through her jeans. Seeing her hurt filled him with fury and he grabbed hold of the cane, ignoring the wicked thorns as they dug deep into his skin.

Blood ran from his hands, but he pulled until they came free and stamped them down, helping Gail back to her feet.

"Your hands. You shouldn't have done that." She pulled a hanky from her pocket and fastened it around his right hand, though she had nothing for the left one.

"I'm okay, let's just keep moving." He wiped the speck of blood from her cheek and ignored the urge to pull her into his arms.

Gail nodded, and they both set off after Nick.

It took them a good 20 minutes to negotiate the overgrown garden. The weeds grabbed and snagged at their clothing, holding them back, cutting their skin, and generally making it hard labor to travel even a few feet. It was the first time it was obvious that Nick was a spirit. He passed easily through anything and looked back frustrated that they were taking so long.

Part of Jesse wanted to tell him to go ahead without them, but he knew if he did that they could lose the priest, and right now they needed his help. Inside he was bubbling with frustration. Everything was taking so long, and they had so little time. From what he could find out about Shelly and Jack, they knew nothing. They were wannabes, rank amateurs. Maybe that would work in their favor. Maybe the ghosts would leave them alone, but somehow, he doubted it. Something inside him said they were in danger and time was not on their side. So, he stamped through the garden rushing as much as he could, but now ensuring that the path was clearer for Gail.

They turned the corner to see Nick stood looking at the house. It appeared he was staring at an elderberry bush. When they arrived at his side they could see the door behind it.

Not only did they have to break down a spirit barrier, they would have to get through the bush as well.

"This is the door?"

Nick shrugged his shoulders.

Jesse clenched his fists and tried to work out what to do. They could break the branches, tear them down with their hands. Elderberry was weak but flexible... it would take time.

"Are there any tools nearby?"

Nick nodded. *Yes, there is a tool shed around the back of the house. There would be a scythe in there which would be adequate for this.*

"Tell me where it is, I'll go fetch it," Jesse said.

Nick shook his head. *You could, however it would take too long. I can fetch it.*

Before Jesse could say anything else, the ghostly priest had gone and he turned to look at Gail.

"He's a ghost. How can he fetch it?" she asked, as she pulled her shirt out from her jeans and ripped a strip off the bottom. She took Jesse's left hand and started to bind it.

"Nick's a very old spirit. He's been around so long that I imagine there isn't an awful lot he can't do. The problem is, the more he materializes, the weaker he will become. Manipulating the material world is very tiring, even for one as old as Nick."

Gail nodded. "I see. So, he may not be there when we need him?"

Jesse didn't want to think about that. He didn't want to think about any of this. He could feel the loathing and despair coming from the house. Waves of darkness broke around him, so strong he could almost see them.

Nick was back and handed the scythe to Jesse. Then he blinked out of existence.

It didn't bother Jesse this time. He understood. While Nick was resting, he would be close, and he would be there when they needed him... hopefully.

The sun was up now, and it made them all feel a little bit better, but the clouds were heavy. Jesse imagined it never got that light around RedRise House. There was so much darkness, he doubted the light could penetrate.

Indicating to Gail to step back, he swung the old-fashioned scythe at the elderberry bush and began to chop it down. As he cut into the tree, the smell, arid, sour, and most distinctive, was strong in the air.

Usually, the smell didn't bother him, it was part of the countryside. But today it seemed so strong and vile. It cloyed in his throat making it harder to breathe. It didn't matter, he kept slashing and slicing and pouring all of his frustration and anger into hacking the tree to pieces. He stopped occasionally to throw away what he had cut down before starting again. The scythe was sharp and deadly and soon made short work of the bush.

Panting and wiping sweat from his forehead, Jesse turned to Gail. "I guess we're ready for Nick again."

Before he could say anything else, Nick appeared in front of him and nodded. The priest looked tired and frightened, but there was also determination and steel in his features. Jesse knew he had to have been tough to come this far without being corrupted.

"Can you get us in?" Jesse asked.

Nick nodded, but stood where he was and reached into his

pocket, drawing out a 3-inch-long silver cross on a chain. He handed it to Gail. *I don't know why, but I want to give you this.*

Gail looked at the cross and then at Nick. Jesse understood her confusion. Would she be able to hold it? Was it real? He had heard about this before and knew that she must take it. Nick was strong and old, and if his intuition was telling him she needed it, then she did.

"Take it," Jesse said.

Gail smiled and reached for the cross. Her smile widened as she clasped the chain, lifting it and putting it around her neck. "Thank you," she said.

Nick nodded and approached the door. He went straight through it without even a hesitation. For a moment, Jesse wondered if he would take his vengeance alone, but before he could voice his concern, he heard the sound of a bolt being drawn back... Nick opened the door.

They were in.

They walked into the room which was completely dark, and as Gail crossed the threshold, the door slammed shut behind them. She turned around and tried to find the handle.

"Jesse, there's no handle. I can't get out."

Jesse switched on a torch and looked where the door should be. It was gone. There was just a wood-paneled wall. The varnish was flaking from the boards, and in places, it was holed with woodworm.

Nick was back at their side. He shrugged his shoulders. *Do not worry about this. As I said, the spirits, the owners of the house forgot this door was here. Because of that, it is hidden, but we can find it if we need it again.*

"Then we can get out?" Gail asked, her voice high and on the verge of panic.

Yes, we can get out whenever we want, Nick said, but he turned quickly to walk into the room.

Jesse believed there was more to it than he was saying. He had come across this before a long, long time ago and it was not as easy as Nick was making out. The chances were that they could get out, but the chances were also that it wouldn't be quick. If they were in a hurry, if they were in trouble... Jesse decided not to say anything. Gail was worried, tired, and it was best if she was confident. They would probably need her talent before too long. If she was self-doubting, it would go a long way to her losing that talent.

As they started to cross the room, they came across bunk bed after bunk bed. The wooden beds were pitiful and rickety. Straw mattresses laid atop some of them, stained, ripped, and full of moths and creeping insects. From some, threadbare blankets draped over the side. These two were stained and stank of something best forgotten. It looked like this had once been a dormitory and Jesse could sense the pain and despair that had lived here. It seeped into him, crushing down on his shoulders, shortening his breath, and weakening his legs. Was this some form of sensitivity? Was he feeling the emotions of the spirits that had once been here, or was it just intuition brought on by the stories he had heard and the terrible state of the room?

Placing their feet carefully, trying their hardest not to make a sound, they walked across the room. The wooden floorboards creaked and groaned as if they were telling of the horrors they had witnessed. In places, he could see stains on the walls and stains on the floor. There was no proof, but Jesse knew they were bloodstains. The children who had lived here had not been happy. They had not been cared for. If these were the same ones that now haunted the place, they would be powerful. They would bring with them their rage and a sense of revenge that they carried from their pitiful lives. Maybe they would no longer believe in salvation or the fact that they could, at last, find peace. That would make them harder to deal with. The easy spirits to send away were those who welcomed the peace, those who understood it. If these children had never seen the goodness in anything, then maybe they would fight to stay on the principle that anything was better than nothing, or even because they feared a hell worse than this.

They crossed the large room and arrived at the door. Jesse came past Nick and listened for a moment.

There was nothing. Normally in an old house there would be creaking, groaning, the sound of the wind in the trees outside, or the wind where it had entered the decrepit building. But RedRise House was as quiet as the grave. It made him wonder if they were already too late.

CHAPTER 20

With Shelly's help, Jack was able to make it across the sacrificial chamber and out of the door. They hobbled along the corridor, as best they could in the dim light. Bit by bit they made their way back to the narrow stairs which would lead them back up and into the house.

We should hurry, Stacey said in both of their minds. *We don't know where they've gone or when they will be back. We have to find a way to get you two out of here.*

"No," Shelly stopped and eased Jack on her shoulder. "We can't leave now. I came here... I came here to free these children... I have to see it through.

You came here hoping to contact me, Stacey said, *and you have. I felt the Ghost Hunters... they are here somewhere... let them deal with it, let me get you to safety.*

Shelly didn't understand why, but she was suddenly filled with white-hot rage. It was as if her sister was trying to rule her life from beyond the grave, and she wouldn't let it happen. It never occurred to her that the spirits might be making her feel this way. That they might be manipulating her. All she could see was that Stacey didn't believe in her, and it hurt. She had sent two of the children to peace, and just thinking about that gave her such a sense of achievement and a sense of pride. It filled her with warmth, filled a hole that had been empty for so long. She could do this. She could free these children and she owed it to them to try. Why couldn't Stacey see this?

"I have to stay. We know something is going on here and this," she waved her free hand to emphasize, "is what I've wanted for so long. I can't just walk away. I can't leave these children suffering in eternal torment... not when I can free them."

Stacey turned in front of them, her eyes went black, her hair fanned out behind her, and she let out a shriek of anger that blasted them with cold fetid air. *I just want you to be safe. Why won't you listen to me?*

Shelly fell back, taking Jack with her. They stumbled, tripped and dropped down into the stone passage. As they hit the floor, shock and pain shot up Shelly's coccyx and she cried out.

"Stacey, what's wrong with you? Are you one of them? Are you evil?"

Stacey deflated in front of their eyes, she was once more the young girl with the sweet face and the constant smile. *I have been here a long time... when I get angry I change. I would never hurt you. I'm not one of them... how could you even say such a thing?*

"Then maybe I should give you peace, too," Shelly said, as tears ran down her face.

"No," Jack said as he pulled her to her feet. "Stacey, I agree with Shelly we have to do something for those children they... there is something about them that is so terrible and so sad... I know they are in pain. If the Ghost Hunters are here, then they will find us soon, but we have time to release at least a few of the children."

Shelly was smiling and confident once more. Knowing Jack was on her side was all she needed. All the fear was forgotten. She had a mission and she was going to see that it was completed.

Stacey nodded, and with her head down, she led them to the stairway.

It was hard work climbing the steep, slippery stone steps as both of them were exhausted. Jack was battered and bruised, Stacey was hurt from her fall. So, they took the stairs agonizingly slowly. Despite her newfound confidence, Shelly worried. The dark passage was super creepy. She imagined a hand hauling them down and back to that chamber. At times she thought she heard footsteps behind them or the children keening in the distance. It took all of her courage to keep her nerve and to keep going.

Jack was tiring too. He had been through so much, but step by step they struggled onward. It seemed to take an age before they finally reached the top. When they did, Shelly hesitated. She expected the door to be locked, but it opened easily and let them out.

As they stepped into the kitchen, they noticed the light. It looked like the power was back on, and the house was behaving once more. It was like stepping into the sunshine after a long dark night.

What do you plan to do? Stacey asked.

169

For a moment Shelly didn't know. The spirits had gone... the children had gone. Could she release them when they weren't even here? Somehow, she doubted it. Then it came to her.

"We will have a séance... and as each child comes to us... we will send it to peace."

Jack nodded. Shelly was so pleased with herself for finally making a plan, she didn't notice the pained expression that crossed her sister's face.

Euphoria surged in Shelly, she had never felt anything quite like it. The excitement, the adventure and of course, the fear. Now it was all compounded because she had come so close... they both had, but they'd survived and come out of the other side. Jack wasn't hurt badly, she wasn't hurt, and she had done some good. Maybe if she talked to some of the children, if she recorded what they said, she could not only set them free... she also could help Rosie. Suddenly it felt like coming here had been the right decision, that it was worth it. Maybe this was all a test and she had passed.

"I want to do this properly," she said as she went across to put the kettle on. The house was fueled by an old wood burning range-cooker, but some time across the years it had been converted to use city gas. It took a few moments to work it out, but she lit the gas and set the kettle on to boil up some water.

"We'll all feel better with a hot drink inside of us." She nodded to her sister and Jack not even thinking that Stacey wouldn't be able to drink, and she turned away before she saw her sister's despair.

"Now that that's sorted, we have a little bit of time. I think we should record this. We can set up some cameras in here, and who knows what good we can do with some of these recordings?"

You should leave, Stacey said. *You both need to leave before they come back. The spirits are powerful... they are angry. They do not want you here.*

"Stacey, I love seeing you, but this is my call. We didn't get hurt. I know how to handle them now. I can help those poor, desperate children."

For a moment Stacey's eyes turned black. She clenched her fists and closed her eyes as if she were fighting back a demon. Fury crossed her features and stayed there, mocking them for a few seconds. Then it was gone, and she looked tired, drawn, and lost. She turned to Jack and pleaded with her eyes, begging him to agree with her, to listen to reason.

Jack shook his head. "I agree with Shelly. She can handle this - she can handle anything."

The temperature in the room dropped 20°. Jack's breathe streamed out before him.

Shelly strolled confidently up to her sister.

"Stop doing this. Why could you never help me, never support me?" She waved a finger in front of the ghost's face.

I have been helping you all this time. When you called me, I was there, I have always been there.

"Then help me do this. Help me make a difference."

I don't want you to join me.

Hot tears flooded Shelly's eyes, and she didn't know what to say. Part of her trusted her sister with her life. *To join me...* for a long time she had wanted to do just that. To let go of this harsh, cruel world and be united with the one person who had always understood her. But though that pain had passed, it still hurt, still caused her gut-wrenching guilt, but she wanted to live. Wanted to have a life with Jack, helping people, and this was an amazing opportunity for her to do just that. Why couldn't Stacey see it?

Maybe she was jealous. Maybe she resented that Shelly had pulled her life back together. Part of her didn't believe she could be so mean. But then, she had been dead six years — who knew how much that changed you? She wanted to ask her why she was doing this, to ask for her support again, but the kettle whistled behind them. Relieved, she whipped around to make the drinks.

Shelly placed three hot coffees on the table and didn't notice the sadness that the third cup caused her sister.

"We should make a plan," Shelly said as she sipped at the scalding drink.

The only plan we need to make is how quickly we can get out of here, Stacey said.

"Oh, Stacey, stop being such an old stick-in-the-mud." Shelly rolled her eyes at her sister and turned to Jack. "She was like this as a child. Always a worrywart, always thinking we would be in trouble if we didn't do the right thing. She would never have any fun unless I pushed her into it."

This is different, Stacey said. *I fear for you both... I fear for your lives.*

Shelly laughed. "Yes, I remember. Remember that time when we went to the fair? Dad said we couldn't go until we'd finished our homework, but that would mean it would have been too late to go. So, I pretended we'd done it and we snuck out. You told us Dad would ground us for a year. It didn't happen. Can you remember the fun we had?"

Shelly waited until Stacey gave the smallest of nods.

With laughter in her eyes, she turned to Jack. "Candy floss got stuck in our hair when we went on the Ferris wheel."

She couldn't help but think of the memory. The two of them had been laughing so much and throwing their heads back, but as the wheel jerked, suddenly the gondola had tipped back and jerked their hands. The candy floss was sent flying over the back of them, but before it dropped, it caught in their hair.

Shelly's had just held there for a moment and then dropped down onto the person below. Stacey's had caught in her long brown tresses and covered it in pink cotton. They had spent the rest of the night trying to pick the sticky mess out of their hair, but it had been fun. They had laughed so much that by the time they got home their sides ached from the effort. It had been one of her favorite memories and as it came back, tears swarmed into her eyes."

That was different. There is danger here. You need to leave. I beg of you, please go now.

Shelly sipped her coffee and tried to ignore the bad feeling in her gut. Stacey seemed genuinely concerned. It had been pretty scary, but that was over now. She had it under control. They had a chance to do some good. She was going to follow it through.

The main thing she had to do was make sure she didn't look scared. If she put out a front of confidence, the ghosts would know and they would respect her. That was what she had to do.

"Let's just drink our drink and then we can set some cameras up and help these poor children go to peace. Then I promise you, I will leave."

Stacey nodded, but she seemed to fade for a moment, and then she was back, now smiling.

"Do you have a plan... which child to release first?" Jack asked.

Shelly hesitated. How would she decide? "I think the children will decide for us."

It's not the children you need to worry about, Stacey said.

Shelly flashed her eyes angrily and was pleased with the look of shock that crossed Stacey's face. Then her sister was gone. One moment she was there the next she wore a look of panic, and she just faded... and was gone.

For a moment, Shelly was devastated. Had she driven her away? She hoped not, but it was too late to worry about that now.

"Hey Stacey, come back. I miss you." It was the nearest she could think of to an apology and she hoped Stacey would take it.

"Those ghost hunters will no doubt be here any minute." Jack finished his coffee and placed his mug smartly down on the table. "Why don't we set up the cameras and get things started before they can steal all our thunder?"

Shelly nodded and took a big drink of her own coffee. It was so hot it scolded her throat, causing her to choke. How on earth could Jack drink it so quickly?

They gathered up the cameras from around the house and set them all up in the kitchen. There was the camcorder, four webcams, and her phone surrounding the table. Shelly was sure that they would capture anything that happened.

Stacey still hadn't returned, and she was worried. Where had she gone? Was she just angry or was it something else?

Since her sister had blinked out of existence, Shelly had been left with a cold, empty feeling inside. It was much like the one she had when Stacey first died. She had learned to cope with that death, learned to carry on, but she had never really recovered. How could she recover from such a thing? Her counselor had told her she had to let go and move on. And in many ways, she had... she had never given up hope of seeing Stacey again. Now to see her for such a short time, and to lose her after something so trivial... it all seemed too much. Maybe that was why her stomach felt like the bottom had dropped out of the world.

Jack finished adjusting the cameras and indicated that he was ready.

Shelly sat at the table, and in front of her were three candles and a plate with a small cake. She lit the candles and nodded to Jack.

Behind him, hiding in the doorway, was a young girl, Alice. She looked around eight with long brown hair and a clean white dress. Furtive eyes flashed back and forth as if she feared being caught. It had been just a short time since she'd left this house. Since she'd put it behind her for hopefully the last time... and here she was, back again. Fear crushed her chest, even though she knew she did not breathe. Jack moved, and she slunk back into the shadows.

Jack switched off the lights. The room was plunged into semi-darkness.

It was like going into a different dimension. There was nothing but shadows and so many places for evil to hide. Shelly shook her head. Why was she thinking like this?

Jack sat opposite her, and they joined hands. Shelly knew that for a séance she should really have three people, but she didn't have three people. They would have to do what they could with what they had. At first, she had set up the Ouija Board, but then she closed it and put it to one side. She didn't know why, but instinct told her they wouldn't need it to draw out the spirits.

It was time, and though she knew she should be excited, she was actually afraid. *Had she bitten off more than she could chew?*

"Are we ready?" Jack asked.

Shelly nodded. If she didn't do this soon, he would think she was frightened and she wouldn't allow that.

"Spirits of the past, we bring you gifts from life into death. Move among us and be guided by the light of this world and visit upon us."

Shelly waited. Across the table, she could see that Jack was starting to shift in his seat. His hands were sweaty, or was it hers? One of them was shaking slightly.

Nothing happened.

She held her breath hoping, waiting...

The candles flickered, shadows leaped across the room, and her heart pounded in her chest. Before she lost her nerve, she repeated the incantation.

"Spirits of the past, we bring you gifts from life into death. Move among us and be guided by the light of this world and visit upon us."

The temperature dropped and her breathe misted before her. Goosebumps rose on her arms, and she could see more mist as Jack exhaled. There was a wonder in his eyes, and his lips parted slightly. He trusted her, he believed in her. Could she do this?

Whispers came from all around them and something cold kissed the back of her neck. The urge to let go and to run was primal, but she kept still... kept as calm as she could.

Then it started. Low at first, just at the edge of their hearing. More a pain than a noise, but she knew what it was... the high-pitched keening that came from the sacrificial wounds in the children's throats.

They were here.

It wasn't the welcome she'd wanted from them, and for a moment she wondered if Stacey was right. Should she just leave?

The keening grew in volume. It grated on her nerves and seemed to strum the bones in her chest. She wanted to cover her ears and to scream at them to stop. But Jack was crushing her fingers as he held her hands so tightly.

"I came here to help you, to free you... why are you attacking us?"

The noise stopped as suddenly as it had started, and Shelly let out a desperate gasp. The room filled with mist, and out of it, one by one, stepped over a dozen children. A few of them looked as old as 14 or maybe 15, but some of them looked as young as 6. There were boys and girls, blondes and brunettes, but all of them looked dirty and malnourished. Their eyes shone like the black pits of hell.

"Who would like to leave here?" Shelly asked, as she stared at the children. Her breath was coming too fast, her chest was tight, and more than anything she wanted to run from the room and never come back. She had been a fool. As soon as they found Jack, they should have left. Now she knew why her sister had abandoned her — Stacey believed she couldn't be helped, and maybe she was right.

The smallest of the children came forward those black eyes looked right through her. His lips were curled back like a feral dog, and every inch of him was tensed for attack.

"I'm here to help you," she repeated.

He faded a little.

She could see the children behind him through his form. It made her feel stronger, more in control. If he was insubstantial then he couldn't hurt her – could he?

A laugh echoed around the room. It was from something much older than the children, much older than her, and it was mean and cruel.

Swallowing, she fought to keep still, to hold her nerve, and to do what she knew was right. *Stacey, if you can hear my thoughts, I need you. Help me.*

Nothing happened. It was time, but she couldn't remember the ritual. All she could do was stare at that child, stare at those eyes, and pray he kept his head level. Right now, if that keening started again... if they raised their heads and showed the terrible gashes in their throats... she didn't think she could survive it and stay sane.

"Are you waiting for something?" Jack asked.

Shelly's throat was so dry, so tight, she didn't think she could talk even if she remembered the words. She shook her head, swallowed, and tried to moisten her lips.

"I'm..." The word was just a croak.

Jack let go of her hands. He broke the circle, got up, and walked across to the sink, returning with a glass of water.

Shelly didn't realize that breaking the circle should have freed the spirits. If she were the one calling them, holding them here, then they would have gone.

She sipped at the water gratefully. At first, her throat was closed so tightly that the water wouldn't go down, and she wondered if she would drown.

Jack put his hand on her shoulder, providing support, comfort, and suddenly she could relax. Suddenly she knew the words.

"In the Name of Jesus, I rebuke the spirit of..." She didn't know the name of the child, but suddenly a name came into her mind, and she spoke it. "Daniel Matthews."

A huge grin came onto the little boy's face, his eyes were no longer black. They were tired and surrounded by bags, but they were a warm walnut brown color. There was hope deep inside of them.

That smile was all the encouragement, all the thanks that she needed. She returned it and nodded to let him know she understood. "I command you leave this place, without manifestation, and without harm to me or anyone, so that He can dispose of you according to His Holy Will."

As she finished the releasing prayer, Daniel stood before her with tears in his eyes. He mouthed the words *thank you*, then turned back to the rest of the children and then he was gone, leaving just a flash of white mist in his place.

Shelly wondered about a girl sitting to one side. This one seemed to be hiding, but watching Daniel leave was like a drug. She felt invincible and excited to help the next child.

"Who would like to be next?" she asked.

But it wasn't a child that stood before her. It was Mr. Duncan.

CHAPTER 21

*P*aralyzed with fear, Shelly couldn't speak, move, or even think. There was something evil about the grey-haired man. It wasn't just the coal black eyes and the way his lips curled back over his teeth.

Now it's your time, he said and floated over toward them.

Shelly looked at Jack. How she wanted to apologize, to get him out of there, but it was too late. She understood that now.

"I'm sorry, Stacey." Turning her eyes to Jack, she squeezed his fingers. "I'm sorry."

"Don't be sorry, fight it." Jack's eyes were full of fear, but he held onto her hands, giving hope and strength.

Shelly nodded, but she didn't know how. The children were all against her and behind them were two cloaked adults. She couldn't see their faces but knew that one would be the other Duncan. The others were simply lost, corrupted souls and she knew that she should pity them, but right now all she felt was fear.

Together, these spirits held the children. Forced them to comply. Made them join with this man. They added to his power, though she doubted it was by choice. Part of her knew that she should release them, that if she did, then she would reduce his power. But, her mouth wouldn't open, the words wouldn't come.

There was one little girl sitting to the side, the one she had seen earlier. She was different, cleaner, and purer. It was something she couldn't put her finger on, but this one wasn't touched by the darkness. She wasn't under their control.

The little girl smiled.

Shelly smiled back and then she heard her voice in her head.

I am Alice, Rosie saved me. I want to help you help my friends. They are not bad children, just trapped, in servitude to evil. Repeat the words of the ritual with me, and we can weaken him.

Shelly nodded.

The man roared, and a wind swelled up inside the kitchen. It pushed Shelly and rocked the chair she was sitting in, but the young ghost came across and stood between her and the man.

Alice began to talk, *In the name...*

Shelly tried to force the words past the lump in her throat. "I... I... In the Name of Jesus, I rebuke the spirit of."

They were reciting the ritual together, talking in sync, and she felt her confidence grow as she heard the spirit's voice in her head. As she got to the name of the child, a little girl stepped forward and the name Claire came into her mind.

No last name came, but somehow, she knew there wasn't one. This poor child had lived her life with just a first name, but at least now she would go to peace.

The little girl looked up and as her eyes cleared, they were the lightest sky-blue, and the smile on her grubby face was worth a million.

"I command you leave this place, without manifestation and without harm to me or anyone, so that He can dispose of you according to His Holy Will."

She clapped her little hands and faded away, leaving just a flash of light before that too was gone.

While she was repeating the ritual, Shelly hadn't noticed the wind but as the child faded, it howled and batted against her. She wondered how long she could hold on.

"Are you okay?" she asked Jack.

He nodded. "You can do this."

Shelly wondered if she could, as she began the ritual again.

The children huddled together, an air of expectation hanging around them, but they seemed less hostile.

"In the Name of Jesus, I rebuke the spirit of Mickey Smith."

A young boy with holes in the knees of his trousers came forward. Once more, the child offered her a smile and a nod of thanks.

Shelly returned the smile. Maybe she *could* do this. "I command you leave this place, without manifestation and without harm to me or anyone, so that He can dispose of you according to His Holy Will."

The wind howled around them and yet somehow, they were

protected, as if they were sitting in a bubble and the spirit couldn't get to them. Shelly looked at Alice, and she nodded.

Taking a breath, it was time to say the ritual again, but before she could start, she heard the sound of shouting in the distance. What, now?

At the sound of voices, Mr. Duncan faded and was gone. The wind dropped in the room, and Shelly let out a sigh of relief.

* * *

"THIS WAY," Nick shouted over his shoulder as he ran down the corridor.

Gail followed. Jesse could see she was excited and looking forward to meeting the spirits, but he still had a nagging feeling about this.

From the outside, he knew they should have traveled the corridor in less than 30 seconds, but the further they ran, the further it seemed they had to go. The spirits were playing with them, and his sense of distress was even stronger.

They needed help, and part of him wanted Gail to contact the spirits of the house, but he knew that wasn't a good idea. Nick was panicking, he should have seen through this but his terror was allowing the illusion to rule. So, as Jesse ran, he calmed his mind and called on his spirit guides. "Guide me, wise ones. Be with me in the dark places and guide me back to the light."

They carried on, running and running, and for long moments nothing happened. Then he felt enveloped in warmth and love. Rose had answered. Would she be able to help them?

"Hey you two, hold up for a minute."

Jesse stopped and closed his eyes. Up ahead he could see the big brindle boxer dog, her pink tongue hanging out, and he could swear she was smiling at him once again. Even in the gloomy light, her tiger-striped coat gleamed and her big brown eyes shone with love.

"What is it?" Gail asked, but as she turned, a smile formed upon her face and Jesse knew that she could see.

Nick came back to them. There was a sense of wonder on his face, and he looked from the dog to Jesse and back again.

Jesse wanted to explain, but he knew that time was short so he nodded at the priest and closed his eyes once more. He could only see Rose with his eyes closed. It was the extent of his gift for now, but that was enough.

"Hey Rose, we need to find Jack and Shelly. They are held here by malicious spirits, and they are in danger. Can you lead us out of this deception?"

Rose nodded her head up and down as if she was saying *yes*, and then she bounced on her feet for just a moment before turning and racing down the corridor.

"Can you see her Gail, Nick?" Jesse asked.

"Yes," they both replied.

"Good. I will follow you, as I don't want to be running down these corridors with my eyes closed."

Gail nodded and started to follow. Nick raised his eyebrows and Jesse shook his head.

"That's the only way I can see her."

As Rose moved down the corridor, the area in front of them

shimmered, and suddenly they were walking out into a large open entrance hall.

There was a staircase on the left and an identical corridor to this one straight ahead, but the dog turned across the open space, glancing back to see that they were following.

It was a big room, dimly lit by a huge chandelier. There was a door on either side and what looked like the front door to the right of them.

Rose went straight across to the door on the left, her paws silent on the hardwood floor while their own feet made more noise the further they walked.

As they came into the kitchen, they felt the temperature drop. Jesse could see Shelly and Jack sat at a table. He let out a sigh of relief because they looked okay, but they weren't his first concern. There was something dark, something evil here, and he could feel it.

He closed his eyes, and there in front of him were almost a dozen ragged and emaciated children. Their eyes were black, their faces feral, and their clothes tattered and old. It looked months since they had bathed and there was something malicious about the way they were staring. Behind them stood two cloaked adults. They wore long, dark sacrificial robes that covered their heads and hid their faces. Between the children and the table was another cloaked figure. Even without any skill, Jesse could feel the malevolence coming from that character. He was the leader. He had the strength here, and he was the one they needed to avoid.

Rose stood in front of them, her legs four square, her head high as she stood guard between them and the danger. Jesse didn't doubt that she would try and help him but his instincts said it wasn't a good idea.

"Thank you, Rose," he said.

She came up to him and whined softly before vanishing.

Jesse wanted to call her back, but he had other things to worry about. They needed to get out of here, and they needed to do it quickly.

He opened his eyes and could see Gail staring at the children. Nick stood, eyes wide, mouth open, and Jesse understood. He was facing down his biggest fear. Afraid that now he was here... a sacrifice would be made.

Shelly and Jack were conducting a séance, and for a moment Jesse was angry. Why weren't they trying to escape? Why were they just sitting there? But then he remembered what he had been like. How much of an addiction spirits could be. How many times had he pushed the boundaries when he was younger? Still, it was time they all left.

"Gail, forget them. We have to get out of here."

Shelly turned and broke the circle. The spirits were still there. What was more, Jesse could see them with his eyes open. They were strong, they had a lot of power, and they were very dangerous.

Jesse approached the table.

"Nick told us you were here," he said. "I'm Jesse, this is Gail and we need to get you out of here, and we need to do it now."

"No," Shelly said. "We have to help the children. We are releasing them one by one, and we really don't need your help."

Jesse knew what was happening. The dark spirit was allowing her some success while it gathered its power. She was being lulled into a false sense of security. Soon, the figure would make its move. They had to escape now before it was too late.

Gail came to his side, a droplet of sweat running down her cheek. It was taking all her skill to keep the dark one out. Jesse felt a surge of pride. The temptation for her to connect with them must be immense, but she had sensed the danger, and she was fighting it.

"Nick," he called.

The priest was staring into space, so afraid that he couldn't move.

Gail nodded. She went to him and reached out. She could touch him, just, and she gently shook him out of his fear. Jesse watched his face clear. He was back with them. Together, they all turned to the table.

"You must leave," Nick said.

"No, not until we have freed all the children." Shelly was adamant, and she turned away from them.

Jesse could see that Gail was sympathetic and that even Nick wanted to help. Both of them could feel the pain of the children, but all he worried about was the living. Once they had escaped the house, they could do the releasing ritual from the outside. And then he saw a young girl peeking out from behind Jack.

She smiled up at him and waved her hand, and then he heard a voice in his head.

I need to talk to you.

Jesse answered instinctively, thinking the words in his own mind. *It will have to wait. We need to get out of here.*

Yes, you do, and I can help. But first I have to tell you something, and I can't do it from outside.

Jesse could hear arguing behind him. He knew the two young ghost hunters wanted to stay and that Gail and Nick wanted them out of here. He knew he should join in, he wanted to help, but he needed to hear what the young ghost had to say. It was a feeling so strong he couldn't explain it.

My name is Alice, she said, filling the gap of his hesitation. *I was here when Rosie came to the house. I had been here a long time. I cannot explain to you what that is like living year after year, decade after decade, century after century. Always bound to evil always forced to bind others. Rosie freed me from this at a great personal cost... I need to help her. Will you give me just a little bit of time?*

"Give me a bit longer to free all of the spirits," Shelly said from the table.

"Yes," Jesse said aloud in answer to Alice's question.

Everyone heard and they all thought that he was giving Shelly more time. It looked like he was staring at the children, when in fact he was looking to their left, but it didn't matter. The decision had been made.

Gail and Nick sat down at the table and joined hands with the two already there. Nick's hand was like cold water, barely there, but he was holding it together as much as he could. They looked across at Jesse.

"Are you going to join us?" Gail asked.

Jesse didn't hear. All he could see was Alice, and all he could hear was what she was saying to him.

Alice had moved around the back of the other spirits. They

189

didn't seem aware of her, and she went across to the corner of the room out of the way.

Will you let me help her? she asked, again.

"I will." Jesse stepped closer to her. *But please be quick.*

Alice nodded. *All I need is for you to give some information to your man who champions for Rosie.*

For a moment Jesse didn't know what she meant, then he understood. She meant Paul Simmons, the solicitor who represented Rosie.

"I don't think information is going to help her."

Alice smiled, but before she could say any more, the wind rose in the room and Jesse staggered on his feet.

Time is short, Alice said, and she tried to reach out to him, but Jesse was confronted by the two cloaked spirits. As they came toward him, he could feel the cold seeping into his bones, freezing the breath in his throat. The darkness that emanated from them was like a weight on his shoulder, pushing him down into a pit of despair.

"No!" he screamed again, as he watched Alice was surrounded by the children.

"Be gone, Satan, inventor, and master of all deceit."

The spirits advanced. The pressure on his lungs was so great that he backed away.

"Be gone, enemy of man's salvation. Unclean and evil beast, hear the Lord's words and be gone."

The cloaked figures approached him and lifted their heads. He could see their faces... gaunt, white, skeletal. They opened their mouths, and darkness like a million flies blasted him, knocking him backward with the scent and taste of rot and corruption.

Jesse was pushed back until he hit the wall.

The children started their high-pitched keening as they closed in on Alice.

"No!" Jesse screamed as he got to his feet and faced down cloaked death. This time he pulled out his Holy Water and splashed them as he recited the prayer. "Christ, God's Word made flesh, commands you. Be gone, Satan, inventor, and master of all deceit, the enemy of man's salvation. Unclean and evil beasts, hear the Lord's words and be gone."

It was working. They were backing from him, but that seemed too easy. So, he splashed more Holy Water. "Be gone from here, be gone. They slunk away, and he ran to Alice. It was too late. With her face twisted in pain, she was pulled back and upward until she faded into the ceiling. She was gone.

Jesse screamed out his frustration, and the children turned to face him.

"Jesse, hold on!" Gail shouted.

He turned around to see the séance in progress.

The cloaked ghost was standing over the table. A darkness seeped from him laying a black mist across the circle.

Jesse's heart missed a beat as he saw them enveloped in that darkness. He knew what was happening, but before he could move more than a couple of paces, the hooded spirit disseminated and became a living black smoke.

It swirled around the table like a murmur of starlings swarming across the dusk sky. This was not a coming together for the common good, but a deadly plague about to attack. The malevolent swarm turned and twisted over each person, choosing, deciding, and then, in less than a heartbeat it turned, and like a swarm of killer bees, it dove down and into the open mouth of Jack.

Jack broke the circle. His head flew back and his eyes turned black.

Shelly screamed out her anguish.

CHAPTER 22

*J*ack was thrown across the room like he had been shot from a cannon and came to a stop almost as quickly. He hung there, in front of the wall, his eyes black, his mouth open. Like a six-foot puppet with all its strings cut, he was suspended 3 feet above the ground.

Shelly screamed and ran toward him.

Jesse tried to grab her arm, but she was too quick and slipped through his fingers. He knew what was happening. The ghost, the controlling spirit in the house, had possessed Jack. It would take him but a few moments to control the body, which was all the time they had... all the advantage. If they acted quickly, maybe, just maybe, they could expel him before he had use of his full powers.

Jesse grabbed for his Holy Water as he raced across the room.

Shelly got there first. She reached up, but just as she did, the spirit took control.

Jack's head turned down, his eyes red now, and the look he gave Shelly was enough to break her heart.

His lips were pulled back from his teeth and he spoke to her in tongues. The old language, the foul language. Jesse couldn't understand it, but he could understand the meaning. It was vile, degrading. Like the rumbling of a sewer, it spewed out of him, telling them how little they were worth.

Jesse grabbed hold of Shelly's arm and pulled her back. She was struggling, but he held on tightly as he threw the Holy Water at Jack's face. It hit square on, and the water burned Jack's skin, causing blisters and bubbles to erupt on the surface.

Shelly bucked in Jesse's arms like an untamed bronco. He held her tightly, waiting for her to calm.

"Stop this!" she shouted. "You're killing him, stop it!"

Jesse grabbed her with both arms and looked her in the eye. He could see the fear, and he could also see guilt. He shook her gently.

"You know what this is, you know what he is, and you know what we have to do."

Shelly nodded, a tear traced slowly down her swollen cheek.

"This is all my fault. I did this to him. this is all my fault."

"No, it's not, but that doesn't matter now. All that matters, is getting us out of here... alive."

Shelly nodded. She looked up at Jack. Jesse could see she was strong and he could feel that she had talent. Maybe with her, Gail, and Nick, they had a chance. Maybe, just maybe.

Gail and Nick were at his side now. They all surrounded Jack.

He hung in the air, staring down at them. Still looking like a puppet and hideously suspended, the possession had not gone well. Apart from the blisters, his face had swollen up and looked like a balloon ready to pop. His eyes bulged out, his lips sat like pink slugs beneath a nose that had shrunk into swollen, vein-striped cheeks. It could happen sometimes, usually, when the subject was fighting. The spirit had to surge into the body with such force that it swelled the recipient. The longer the possession was held, the more damage would be done. Jesse knew they had to exorcise Jack quickly or he may be permanently changed. The longer the spirit stayed in his body, the more power he would have. It was a race for Jack's life, and possibly for their own.

Jesse grabbed Shelly's arm and nodded at Nick. "I need you to do something for me."

Though he knew time was short, he waited for them to acknowledge that they had understood. He had been in situations like this before and knew that you had to take things slowly and calmly with people who were under such stress.

Shelly was holding on, but she was terrified and full of guilt.

Nick looked close to going into shock. Jesse didn't know whether that was possible for a ghost, but he guessed it must be. If things got too bad, the priest would either freeze, or he would dematerialize and leave them there, alone with this hell going on around them. Jesse couldn't let that happen... he needed them on his side.

What had only been microseconds seemed to take forever, but Shelly was the first to nod her head, Nick followed suit.

Gail stood next to them and added her own nod of agreement.

"I need you to remove the spirit's power. Shelly, have you been using a releasing prayer?"

Shelly nodded.

"Good. I want you and Nick to continue. Do it as quickly as you can and free as many souls from this house as you can."

"But Jack J... J... Jack... I have to save Jack."

Jesse squeezed her shoulder and gave her his most winning smile. Keeping calm, keeping her calm, was a big part of them getting out of this. Almost as big a part as getting rid of as many of these ghosts as they could.

"I know," Jesse said. "I have seen how skilled you are at this. The house, the children, they are in tune with you. You are the right one to do this, but I am the right one to exorcise Jack. Help me, help him."

Shelly nodded and went back to sit at the table.

For a moment, Nick stood in front of Jesse, he worried that the priest would leave. that it was too much for him. Shelly could probably do this alone, but with the power that Nick's presence gave her, it would be a lot easier, a lot quicker.

"I know you're frightened," Jesse said. "I also know you have a big heart and that you can do this. Help us, my friend, for we need you."

Nick nodded, and started to walk toward the table. Jesse could see that he was fading and he hoped that Nick had the energy to stay just a little longer.

Jack roared, and a wind rose in the kitchen. It pushed them

all back, but seemed to surge toward Nick. He was knocked off his feet and sent hurtling through the air. He hit the kitchen wall opposite Jack, and was pinned there.

Shelly screamed and ran toward him.

"Stop!" Jesse shouted. "Release the children."

For a moment she hesitated, looking at Jack and then to Nick and back again.

"Release the children!" Jesse shouted, but he didn't have time to see if she obeyed. He had to get to Nick for the children, and the remaining adult spirits were surrounding him.

Jesse expected him to leave, to fade, and to lose all his power, but Nick held his head high. Despite the fact that he was pushed back against the wall, he began to chant the releasing prayer.

"In the Name of Jesus, I rebuke the spirit of Ada Johnson."

Jesse could hear Nick and he saw a young girl peel away from the group, but the rest of them were approaching the preist with hate in their eyes. Their lips were pulled back, their teeth were bared, and they raised their hands, holding them out like clubs and claws.

Jesse looked behind him. Shelly was going to Jack. He understood why, but it was the wrong move. Now he had a choice: help Nick or Shelly. For a moment he wavered, but his instincts pulled him toward Nick. As he turned, he saw Gail head toward Jack. He prayed she would be in time and that she would be safe. For now, all he could do was fight the wind and try to help the priest. The ladies would have to fend for themselves.

CHAPTER 23

*G*ail was knocked from her feet as the wind picked up. It sent her tumbling back until she hit the kitchen cabinets. The impact jarred her spine and crushed the air from her lungs. But she gathered her strength and clawed her way back to her feet. They had to take control of this. She could see Jesse crawling to his feet and turning to help Nick.

Out of the corner of her vision, she saw Shelly approach Jack, or what remained of him. The face was no longer that of a sweet young man, rather something swollen and hideous with red eyes filled with malevolence.

Gail could feel Shelly's power. She was like her, and for a moment she didn't know what to do, but then Jesse caught her eye and it came to her. She had to help Shelly, to keep her from Jack and then help her release the children. She would have to rush.

Shelly approached Jack, and there were tears in her eyes. The look on her face reminded Gail of a victim of trauma. She was refusing to believe what she saw. She had closed down, shut out the truth, and only saw what she wanted to.

Gail could hear Nick repeating the releasing prayer.

"I command you leave this place, without manifestation and without harm to me or anyone, so that He can dispose of you according to His Holy Will!" Nick shouted.

As Gail fought the wind and made her way toward Shelly and Jack, she was aware of a feeling of joy. Amongst all the darkness it was like sunshine after a storm — she understood. One of the children had been sent to peace. It was so tempting to look, to watch, but she had to get to Shelly before it was too late.

Shelly was so close now. She reached up to Jack, a tender hand offering comfort.

Jack screamed a litany of jumbled words, guttural, coarse, and unfathomable. His arms had dangled at his sides, but now they shot up, jerked by the spirit puppet master. The right hand lashed out at Shelly, turning and raking his nails across her face. Deep welts ripped across her skin, weeping blood as he pulled his left hand back for another try.

Shelly was knocked back by the force, but the wind changed and held her in place. Despair filled her eyes, followed by disbelief as she waited for the second blow.

Gail charged... hitting Shelly with her shoulder, she forced her out of the way and stood before the face of evil.

"Be gone foul scum!" she shouted as she tossed Holy Water at the grotesquely swollen face. "Leave this place and go back to the hell hole you came from."

Jack mocked her with laughter that boomed toward her with the force of a jet engine blast. It almost took her from her feet, but she stood her ground. Gritting her teeth, she battled the wind and threw more Holy Water... then it came to her. The crucifix. Reaching around her neck, she took hold of the cross that Nick had given her. The wind dropped, and she walked toward Jack.

"Be gone foul beast!" she shouted. "You are not welcome here, not invited. I cast you out with the power of the crucifix and the Lord's words."

Jack's eyes flew open and blood leaked from the corners, running down his swollen cheeks.

Gail never used the proper words. She said what came to her and put all her intention behind it. It worked... was working.

Jack began to convulse. His body dropped to the floor and lay there writhing and struggling.

Shelly ran to him. Gail pulled her away. "You will help him by releasing the children."

Shelly's eyes pleaded, and for a moment she screamed hysterically, struggling and fighting in Gail's arms like a wounded bobcat.

Gail pulled her into an embrace. Pinning her arms to her side, she held her and talked calmly. "It's all right. Relax, let go. We will save him. Be calm."

Shelly tried to pull away, but her strength had gone. She crumpled against Gail's shoulder and sobbed.

Gail held her close and waited for her to calm. "Trust me," she whispered.

Shelly's tears gradually subsided and Gail pulled back. "Help us, help him by releasing the children."

Shelly rubbed the tears from her eyes and nodding, she ran to the table.

* * *

JESSE WATCHED Gail go after Shelly, and he turned back to find the priest surrounded by feral children.

Pressed back against the wall, Nick was terrified. Desperate to keep out of the spirits' grasp, he cowered back, flattening himself just out of their reach.

Jesse understood. The malevolence of the spirits just touching Nick would leach his strength. But if enough of the children grabbed him, they could pull him from here, could take him away, and Jesse feared for where Nick would be sent.

Tiny hands reached out for him. The older ones were clawing and pulling at his clothes.

"Get away from him!" Jesse shouted and threw Holy Water on the backs of the children.

They turned, more from shock than anything else, it gave Jesse an opportunity. Quickly he darted around them and placed himself between Nick and the crown of spirits.

As they turned back, they brought a blast of icy air. The cold dampened his morale and weakened his knees. The urge to rub at his arms and to huddle for warmth was overwhelming, but he shook it off and let out a big breath. The air misted before him and he froze in its thrall for a moment.

The smaller children fixed him with their black eyes. Their heads back, the wounds at their throats flapped and mouthed at him. Jesse wanted to scream at them, wanted to release them, but for long moments he couldn't move. Then he gasped for a desperate breath, and it released him from the paralysis of terror.

"Be gone from here!" he shouted as he threw Holy Water on them.

The children stepped back and hissed at him. The sibilant sound slithered between them and made his skin crawl. All he wanted to do was move them back, to give Nick time to release them. But would it work?

With teeth bared, they hissed, snarled, and growled, inching toward him, crowding him, pushing him back toward Nick.

Jesse held his ground. Feeling for some weakness, he was wishing he was sensitive, wishing he could read them like Gail could. It was no use, and as the children crowded closer, he noticed that two of them, teenagers, a girl and boy, were talking, whispering, colluding. What were they up to?

"Release them, Nick" Jesse shouted — nothing happened.

The priest cowered against the wall. His jaw slack, his hands shaking in front of him, and his eyes... his eyes were somewhere else. For centuries he had tried to avoid this. Had relived it over and over again, and now here he was right back in the center. Jesse knew that if they didn't regain control, then all of them would be sacrificed. They would join the undead in this evil house and would be a reminder of Nick's failure for all eternity.

That wasn't going to happen. He wouldn't let it. Gail wouldn't let it.

"Snap out of this Nick, we need you."

A Latin prayer came into Jesse's mind, and he began to recite it. Many years ago, his grandparents had taught him to go with his instincts. Even if his logical mind told him one thing, he should always follow his intuition. Right now, his logical mind was telling him to release the children, but his gut was saying something else.

Keeping an eye on the teenage whisperers, he went with it. "Pater noster, qui es in caelis, sanctificetur nomen tuum."

The pressure eased. Until it did, he hadn't noticed how hard it had been to breathe, to stand upright, to be here. But as he recited the prayer, the air became lighter, clearer, and his mood lifted.

"Adveniat regnum tuum. Fiat voluntas tua, sicut in caelo et in terra."

Behind him, Nick began the releasing ritual, "In the Name of Jesus, I rebuke the spirit of Jonas Peters."

A young boy stepped forward. The black melted from his eyes leaving them a warm blue, and the smile beneath it filled Jesse with hope.

"I command you leave this place, without manifestation and without harm to me or anyone, so that He can dispose of you according to His Holy Will," Nick continued.

The little boy wiped tears from his grubby cheeks and did a little bow before fading in a flash of light.

Jesse had never seen anything so beautiful. While he watched it, he took his eye off the teenagers. It was all they needed. The girl pulled a knife from within her apron and rushed toward Nick.

"No!" Jesse screamed, and he dived into her path. Everything slowed down. He could hear Nick reciting the prayer.

Why doesn't he help me?

The girl was moving too quickly. The knife held out, shining brightly and deadly. Jesse knew that her path would take her straight at him and he didn't doubt that the knife was real. Deadly. It would slice into him, kill him, and still, Nick made no attempt to help.

"In the Name of Jesus, I rebuke the spirit of Elizabeth Smith," Nick spoke calmly.

Jesse wanted to scream, *hurry, help, damn you, Nick!*

In but an instant, the girl stopped. One moment she was flying toward him, brown hair fanned back, eyes black and full of hate, lips pulled back from bared teeth. And the knife… all he could see was the knife.

Then she stopped, hovering for a moment while her eyes lightened down to a chocolate brown. The hatred dropped from her face and was replaced with love. The knife vanished from her fingers.

"I command you leave this place," Nick said as he came up and placed a cold hand on Jesse's shoulder. "Leave it without manifestation and without harm to me or anyone, so that He can dispose of you according to His Holy Will."

The girl smiled and then she, too faded to a speck of light and then to nothing.

The rest of the children stepped back. Jesse couldn't decide if it was fear or wonder on their faces, but for a moment he could breathe.

"We don't have long," Jesse called. He could sense evil building, and he wondered if they would have the strength to stand against it.

CHAPTER 24

The darkness was growing, spreading. The children turned, and like androids, returned to their master.

Jesse scanned the room and his eyes rested on Jack and Gail.

She was standing in front of him, reciting the Lord's Prayer and sprinkling him with Holy Water. He was no longer on the ground but stood before her, and whatever possessed him, was gaining in strength. He was controlling the other spirits, and Jesse knew that time was running out. They should get out of here, but right now they couldn't. The Jack puppet master was too strong.

Sweat ran down Gail's face, strain showed in the set of her jaw, the fatigue of her shoulders. She was failing and desperately needed his help, but before Jesse could join her, he had to protect Nick and Shelly.

"Come with me," he said, as he grabbed some rope and salt from his bag and pulled Nick to the table.

"Sit."

Nick sat down opposite Shelly.

Shock had frozen her solid and leached the color from her cheeks. They would deal with that later but at least for now, he could give them a modicum of safety.

Quickly, Jesse laid a salt circle around the table. The spirits would not be able to cross it, including Nick, and he saw worry and a touch of betrayal cross the priest's eyes.

Jesse shook his head. He had trapped him here, which was cruel, but he believed the man was strong. That he could face the coming terrors. He had to... they needed him.

Nick's eyes pleaded for a moment longer, but then he nodded.

"You will be fine," Jesse said, and turned to Shelly. "Shelly, Shelly!"

She looked up and blinked back her tears."

"We will save Jack... but we need your help."

She nodded.

"You will be protected inside the circle. We need you to release these children, reduce the spirit's power. Jack needs that more than anything, so no matter what happens, **do not** cross that salt line.

She nodded and blinked away her tears.

"The spirits cannot cross it, but they may try to breach it. Use this to keep the line and keep reciting that releasing prayer."

He handed Shelly the salt and held eyes with her for just a

moment until she nodded, and then he turned to face the wrath of the Demon before him.

Gail was being pushed back, slowly but surely. Like a wind, it was forcing her to slide across the slate floor. Back and back she slid, and with each inch, her power over the exorcism failed.

Jesse came up next to Gail and took her hand. It stopped the backward motion, and a look of fury crossed Jack's swollen face.

Gail squeezed his fingers, and together they began to work on exorcising the spirit.

"I cast you out, unclean spirit, in the name of our Lord, Jesus Christ, be gone from these creatures of God."

Jack's spat at them. The spittle burned like acid, but they wiped it from their faces, from their hands, and continued praying.

"Christ, God's Word made flesh, commands you. Be gone, Satan, inventor, and master of all deceit!" Jesse was almost screaming the words as the kitchen filled with a hurricane-like wind. It tried to knock them off their feet, and for a moment Jesse was sent flying backward. Gail caught his wrist and held him as he struggled to maintain his feet.

"The enemy of man's salvation," she shouted.

Jesse joined in, "Unclean and evil beast, hear the Lord's words and be gone."

***The children had surrounded the table. They were trying to get to Shelly and the priest, but they couldn't cross the line. Like animals, they leaped at it, screaming, wailing and shouting but each time they threw themselves, they bounced back, repelled as if they hit an invisible barrier.

Nick and Shelley were repeating the releasing prayer. "In the Name of Jesus, I rebuke the spirit of Jonathan Potter. I command you leave this place, without manifestation and without harm to me or anyone, so that He can dispose of you according to His Holy Will."

One of the children stopped and dropped to his knees. From wild animal to sweet baby, he changed in an instant and gave them a look of such apology.

Shelly wiped tears from her eyes as she smiled at him and then he was gone.

Jesse knew it was happening, but he had to concentrate on the battle in front of him.

The wind pushed at them, and it took every bit of strength they had to battle against it. Screaming the exorcism was like whispering into a storm - useless. Jesse could see that Gail was exhausted. They had to do something, but what?

A picture whipped through the air and caught Gail above the eye. She dropped to the floor. Without her strength, the Jack puppet was able to advance.

"No!" Jesse screamed as he threw himself in front of her. "Keep away from her you bastard! Keep away!"

Jack's face looked as if it would rip as it broke into a smile, and he pulled out a knife. Eight inches of death slashed through the air as he walked toward them. There was confidence in his step. Gloating, he took his time, enjoying the terror he caused.

Jesse reached down and checked Gail's pulse. She was alive, but for how much longer? They had tried everything... had given it their all. They were losing. Tears formed in his eyes as he looked down at the sweet face of the woman he loved. He had brought her into this. He knew this day may come. The one when he failed. When the spirits were too strong.

"I have to leave you, to give it all I have." Gently he moved a lock of brunette hair from her forehead. He kissed her skin and as he did, she started to stir. He pulled her up to a sitting position and stroked her hair back. Jack was getting closer. "Can you walk?"

"Not yet," her voice was weak and shaky.

Jesse pulled her to the side of the kitchen and was about to walk away when she handed him the crucifix that Nick had given her.

"He's afraid of this," she whispered, and closed her eyes.

Panic, like a trapped bird, clawed for escape inside Jesse, but he had to leave her. If he didn't beat this evil, then they all died. With the crucifix in one hand, he grabbed the rope and Holy Water, an idea coming to his mind.

Quickly, he spread the rope out and sprinkled it with Holy Water while reciting a blessing, "Bless this rope with righteous power; imbue it with Your favor, strengthen it as a shield, a barrier to evil."

Glancing back, he could see Jack grinning. Red eyes, mouth impossibly wide, leaking spittle as he came closer. Jesse cowered back, covering Gail, protecting her and waiting.

The spirit laughed. The sound boomed around the room, spraying him with fetid breath that stank like a week-old corpse.

Jesse waited just a moment more and then he sprang to his feet and threw the rope.

"In the name of the Lord Jesus Christ, bind this spirit and hold him."

CHAPTER 25

*T*he spirit roared and thrashed and screamed at him in the ancient tongue. The one forgotten. The one corrupted.

Jesse couldn't understand the words, but they hurt his ears, made him want to cover his head and cut out the sound.

Still, the spirit roared and thrashed, but it hadn't come closer. The rope was working. For the first time in a while, Jesse had the upper hand. He glanced at the table. The children were still circling, testing the salt line but there were less of them. Shelly and Nick looked strong. They held hands and recited the releasing prayer and as he watched, another child broke from the group and transformed into a thing of beauty, of innocence and finally, of peace.

Jesse wanted to watch, to clap and cry for joy, but a scream of torment turned him back. Jack's face was morphing, changing back to the sweet young man he was and then into a thing of evil. One moment young and in agony, the next old and corrupt. Grey hair topped a putrid bag of evil that enjoyed the torment it was inflicting.

The old spirit was fighting... Jesse was going to end that fight. He took the crucifix in his left hand and the Holy Water in his right, and he approached the spirit.

"Pater noster, qui es in caelis, sanctificetur nomen tuum."

The old man's eyes widened as he saw the crucifix. He tore at the rope, but it burned into his flesh, singeing his hands and blistering his face. Then he changed, and was Jack.

"Help me," he cried. "Get this off me. It burns, please help me." Tears ran from his eyes. Tears of blood traced twin rivers down his face.

Jesse stepped forward and held out the crucifix. Jack's eyes were wild with fear, but Jesse pushed it against his forehead. It burned, smoked, and he could smell the singeing flesh, but he held it there.

The old man was back, and gnashing with his teeth, he tried to bite Jesse, but it was all to no avail. The crucifix held him. Jesse could see the spirit giving in, fading.

"Adveniat regnum tuum. Fiat voluntas tua, sicut in caelo et in terra," he shouted, gasping for breath. "Panem nostrum quotidianum da nobis hodie, et dimitte nobis debita."

A feral scream broke Jesse's concentration, and he turned just in time to see the smaller of the cloaked adults running for him. The hood was back and he could see a dead-eyed, old woman. Her teeth bared as she charged into him.

As the spirit hit, Jesse was sent flying. The contact was so cold it froze his shoulder and arm. His fingers opened, and he saw the crucifix flying through the air.

He hit the kitchen cabinets hard with the small of his back and slumped down to the floor. Pain slammed into him like a train, and for a moment he could think of nothing more.

The woman was coming for him. She swirled into a mist and crossed the ground in an instant, then threw out her hand.

Jesse knew what she wanted to do. That arm would be ice cold. It could go through his body and then crush his heart. To a coroner, it would look like he had suffered a heart attack, but it would be all her. She would stay incorporeal until she was inside his chest and there was nothing he could do. The crucifix was just out of his reach, and he had dropped his Holy Water. Maybe he could move, but he could see from the look on her face that she was expecting that.

"Et ne nos inducas in tentationem, sed libera nos a malo. Amen!" he shouted. Just as she was on him, he threw himself to the left, but he felt her hand like a shiver pass into his chest.

Then she dissipated, and Nick landed on the floor at Jesse's feet.

"Nick." Jesse reached down to take his hand and help him up, but he passed straight through the priest.

I have to go for a while. Nick shrugged. It was a sad, but not frightened gesture. *That took all my remaining strength. I won't be here if you ne...*

He faded away, becoming more and more translucent until there was nothing left.

Jesse growled as he jumped to his feet. He wanted to see if he could call the priest back, but there wasn't time for that. The man had saved him at great cost. He just hoped that she hadn't taken Nick with her, but it didn't matter now...

they had to finish this. He hoped that Nick had simply exhausted himself and that he hadn't been taken into the darkness.

Shelly was within the circle reapplying salt to the line where she must have let Nick free. There were only 6 children remaining and one of the adult spirits. They all looked beaten, though they made a weak attempt to cross salt the line.

Jesse grabbed the crucifix and walked back to Jack. His face was once more swollen and red. Blood vessels had burst in his cheeks, and his mouth had split at the corners. Things were going from bad to worse.

Jesse threw Holy Water onto him and held up the crucifix. He saw the panic in the man's eyes and at the same time, a vindictive need for revenge.

He had to move fast, or the spirit would shred Jack and simply leave.

Jesse marched closer until he could put the crucifix on his forehead once more. The body beneath him singed and shook, convulsing beneath his hand.

"I cast you out, unclean spirit, in the name of our Lord, Jesus Christ, be gone from this creature of God."

The body beneath him bucked so hard he feared it would break Jack's spine, but he kept the crucifix pushed into his forehead. It burned, Jack shrieked, but Jesse didn't ease up. Spirits were tricky; he had to be sure it was gone.

"Be gone, spirit of Satan, inventor, and master of all deceit, the enemy of man's salvation. Unclean and evil beast, hear the Lord's words and be gone."

Jack dropped to the floor, convulsing. His heels knocked on the hard tiles, and his body twisted and shook.

A hand touched Jesse's shoulder. He turned to see Gail, and a wave of relief strengthened him.

"Our Father who art in Heaven, hallowed be thy name," Gail started softly, but her voice gained volume as she continued. "Thy Kingdom come. Thy will be done on earth as it is in Heaven."

Jesse repeated the Latin exorcism alongside her. Pater noster, qui es in caelis, sanctificetur nomen tuum."

On the floor, the spirit shrieked and thrashed. Blood was leaking from Jacks eyes and running down his cheeks. Then it was the old man again. He laughed and rose to his feet. "You will never beat me."

The rope held him.

"We've heard it all before," Jesse said. Drawing back his arm, he punched the spirit in the face, knocking him backward.

Gail advanced on him. "Give us this day our daily bread, and forgive us our trespasses."

Jesse advanced on him holding the crucifix. "Adveniat regnum tuum. Fiat voluntas tua, sicut in caelo et in terra."

The spirit backed away from them, morphing and convulsing like an ever-changing rubber man.

"As we forgive those who trespass against us, and lead us not into temptation, but deliver us from evil." Gail followed him.

"Panem nostrum quotidianum da nobis hodie, et dimitte nobis debita nostra sicut et nos dimittimus debitoribus nostris." Jesse stepped closer.

"For thine is the Kingdom, and the power, and the glory, forever and ever, Amen."

"Et ne nos inducas in tentationem, sed libera nos a malo. Amen."

They had pinned the spirit in the corner of the kitchen, his back against the cooker. Fear crossed his face, for there was nowhere else to go.

Jesse put the crucifix against his forehead. "I cast you out and send you back to hell."

Jack threw his head back. Black smoke erupted from his mouth with such force that it tossed Jesse and Gail across the kitchen like rag dolls.

They landed hard on the tiles and turned to see Jack collapsed on the floor as the smoke surrounded the cooker before driving down into the floor, accompanied by the sound of an explosion. It shook the house as it burst through the tiles and traveled down, and down, to wherever it came from.

Jesse got up and pulled Gail to her feet.

"It's over," she said. "We beat him."

Before Jesse could reply, a black cat streaked into the kitchen, its hair singed and still smoking.

Jesse understood. He knew they had very little time.

CHAPTER 26

*S*helly raced to Jack, dropping to her knees at his side. "Jack, oh my God Jack are you..." Gently she stroked his forehead.

"We have to get out of here," Jesse called, as the cat skittered around the room, leaving behind the scent of burning fur. No one was listening to him. Gail had gone to help Shelly. They were helping Jack to his feet.

"I'm all right," he said, as they eased him into a chair.

Jesse felt a moment of relief. Jack would survive, traumatized and who knows what damage had been done to his face, but he would survive if they got out of here. His eyes followed the cat as it raced around the room. The remaining children were trying to keep out of its way. They zig-zagged around as if they were drunk. It was like crazy pinball, and he had to bite back a manic laugh as hysteria nearly took him.

"Damn it, we have to leave now," Jesse called again.

The cat made one final piteous meow before racing into the

wall and disappearing into it.

Above them, the sound of piano keys jarring out of tune floated down through the empty house, and Jesse's sense of urgency kicked up even more. They had banished the spirit, but it hadn't given in. It planned to kill them all, and he knew how.

"We have to leave," he said, as he gently touched Gail on the shoulder.

She winced; they would both be bruised tomorrow, but if they got out now, they would have a tomorrow.

"I'm okay," Jack said. "I could see everything, feel everything, including the joy as the children left. I think we should release the rest of them."

Jesse tried not to wince at the stretch marks and saggy skin around his eyes and mouth. His face looked as if it was too large for his skull. "Yes, yes, we should," Jesse said pulling Gail to her feet. "But from outside."

"There's no urgency now." Shelly shook her head and shrugged her shoulders. "Let's just get it over and finished and maybe I can try to call my sister."

"We have to go," Jesse said, and tried to pull Gail.

"Damn it, Jesse, why?"

"Can't you smell it?" He pleaded with her, but before she could answer, another ghost appeared in front of Shelly.

The girl was younger, but the facial features were the same; they must have been twins.

Shelly let out a gasp. Fresh tears streamed from her eyes. "Stacey, I'm so sorry," she cried.

Me too, but we have to leave, and we have to leave now. Can't you smell the gas? The voice was in all of their heads.

She turned and pointed.

A flame flared on the range, and that was when the smell of gas became overwhelming.

They all stood at once just as the gas caught fire and sent a ball of blue light across the kitchen. It missed them, but the walls were burning. The kitchen door slammed shut.

Urgency took over, and they followed Stacey to the door. A blast of wind knocked them back. It was hard to stand on the slate floor, but they pushed their shoulders into the wind and walked into the storm.

The wind whipped up the flames. They curled at their backs like an angry beast, snapping and reaching. Like a living monster, the fire wanted to consume them, to pull them in and to keep them here forever.

Stacey passed through the door easily. Jesse reached for the handle as the ladies helped Jack. It wouldn't turn -wouldn't budge. He kicked at the door, cursing and shouting, for he knew there was no time to release it by ritual. His Holy Water was gone, and the flames were curling around toward them.

Stacey came back through. *Follow me.*

"We can't," Jesse said. "Can you free the door?"

A look of horror dropped her jaw. She tried to speak, but no words would come.

"Concentrate," Jesse said. He knew Nick would be able to do this, but he had practiced for generations. "Just try."

Stacey nodded and reached out to touch the door. Her hand passed straight through it.

The fire roared in triumph. It had skirted around the kitchen following the walls and was almost on them. Overhead it was eating into the ceiling, and smoke filtered down in big black clouds that curled toward them, herded by an army of flames.

Stacey tried again, but her hand passed through.

It could take ages for her to do this even under the best of circumstance. She had to control her form enough to touch the door, but stay enough of a spirit to fight the ghostly force that held it locked. With the panic and fear she must be feeling, it would be impossible to do this in time.

"Nick, help us!" Jesse shouted, but it was ineffectual against the roar of the fire.

He searched the room for another exit and spotted the window behind the sink. The range cooker was close to that, but the fire had fanned out so ferociously that the area around the cooker was the least affected.

"This way!" he shouted, but no one heard. They were staring at the door and then glancing back as the fire consumed everything in its path.

Jesse shook Gail and pulled Jack from the two girl's' arms. Shelly stared at him, her blank eyes filled with flames from the fire. He pointed at the window and concentrated his energy. "Stacey, help me get them to the window."

Stacey nodded and took Shelly's hand. *Come with me, we can get out of here.*

Jesse dragged Jack across to the window and leaned him into

Gail's arms. Shelly and Stacey were there too, and Shelly helped to hold him up.

The window was a good size, Georgian, the type with small panes of glass interspersed with wood. The wood looked rotten, but he doubted he could break it without doing serious damage to his hands. There was nothing to help, but then he spotted a chair. It was just at the edge of the flames, burning slightly, but if he could get it, then it would work.

"No!" Gail screamed, as he started to race at the chair.

The flames moved like a living beast, licking around to cover the chair and to wash over him. Jesse stumbled back, patting at the flames that licked at his shirt. He knew he would be burned, but not badly - at least not yet.

The flames pulled back as if taunting him, and he readied himself to burst forward and grab the chair.

Shelly coughed, and he could feel the smoke in his own lungs. If the flames didn't kill them, the smoke soon would.

Once more he shot forward, but the flames soared through the air like a red-hot tiger of death, and he was engulfed within their fiery heat. The sensation of burning consumed him, but he tried to make that final stretch. Just as his fingers touched the chair, he was blasted back and sent tumbling across the room.

Stunned for long moments, he came to with Gail smacking his head to put out the flames that burned in his hair.

The pain was more than he could imagine, like acid had been poured over his face, and yet he knew the damage was minor. It didn't matter, they were all coughing now, and soon it would be too late. They would die here. He didn't know what else to do.

CHAPTER 27

*J*esse hauled himself to his feet and ran for the chair. It was surrounded by flames, but he had to try. After the first step he was yanked back. Gail had hold of his arm, and he was too weak to pull himself free.

Her eyes looked up at him, pleaded with him, as a single tear traced a route down her cheek. What could he do? Stifling a cough, he searched the room. There was nothing to use. Nothing that could break the window, but he had to try. Ripping off his T-shirt, he ignored Gail's gasps. The pain in his shoulder and back were intense, and he knew he was burned, but that didn't matter. Gail was coughing. Jack and Shelly were coughing.

Maybe if he climbed onto the counter, he could kick out most of the glass and push the rest out with his arm wrapped in the shirt. He had no doubt it would lacerate his skin, but that was better than dying of smoke inhalation, or God forbid, in the terrible flames.

The wind gusted in the house, and the flames were licking at their backs. Hungry, greedy and all-consuming, they would be on them soon.

Before he could jump onto the counter, a flaming chair appeared out of the fire. It slid across the floor surrounded by smoke, and came to a stop just before him. Stacey, a huge smile on her face, stood just behind it. She had calmed herself enough to push the chair, but it was too late to leave via the kitchen door... flames now blocked that route.

Shelly tried to go to her sister, but Jack stumbled as she left him, and Gail rushed to her side. Together, they held him upright. Their hands covered their mouths to slow down the smoke, but the room was filling up fast.

Jesse wrapped his T-shirt around his hands and grabbed hold of the chair. It was hot, but not enough to burn, and he swung it at the window. The first time it bounced back, and he had to bite back a groan. How much longer did they have?

Again, he raised the chair, but this time he slammed it, feet first, into the glass. Four separate pains shattered and the ensuing rush of air fed the fire at their backs.

Again, Jesse swung the chair at the window. This time at an angle, and one of the wooden cross struts broke. Stopping for a fit of coughing, he could feel the smoke in his lungs. Could feel his brain wanting to shut down. Telling him to sleep. He could feel the bruises and burns on his body. How much more could he take?

Holding his breath, he fought off the cough and smashed the window again. The gap was almost big enough. So, he bashed the chair in a circular motion within the window, clearing the glass.

"You first," Gail shouted.

"No, you and Shelly go first. I can help Jack out and you can catch him."

They nodded and leaned Jack against the counter. Then Gail helped Shelly climb up, and she maneuvered backward through the gap. The fire roared with rage and the spirits of the children and remaining adults surged forward.

"We will help you," Jesse called

The children stepped back and surrounded the two adults. They were a terrifying bunch, and he hoped that this would keep them busy for just a little longer.

He lifted Gail onto the counter, and she climbed out. The sweet air from outside was like an oasis in a desert, almost too good to be true.

Gail dropped to the floor, and he could just see hers and Shelly's head and shoulders. They held up their arms, ready for Jack.

Jesse picked him up in a fireman's lift and put him on the counter. Before he could climb up himself, Jack made his way to the window. He crawled through, but as he did, his arm caught on a rogue bit of glass. Blood poured from the wound, and Jesse reached up to free his flesh.

"Bind it quickly," he said, and tossed his T-shirt out of the window.

Now it was his time, and yet he felt a strange compulsion to stay behind. Something was undone, but he didn't know what. He climbed onto the surface, turned around and dropped down. The ground gave beneath his feet, and it was all he could do to stay standing.

Looking back, he could see the children standing in front of the fire. Their faces were pleading and trusting. Behind them, the fire reared up to the ceiling and sucked up all the air.

"Get back and start releasing the children," he shouted.

"Jesse!" Gail screamed.

"Go, I'm right behind you."

He watched as they started to run and then he eased himself away from the wall. Shaky legs didn't want to hold him, but he knew he had to run. The house was going to explode; he could feel it. Taking a breath, he took one last look back, and there was Alice, watching him.

Jesse stopped, but it was too late. He had to go, so he ran and ran. As he got past the garden he could hear Gail, Shelly, and Stacey all reciting the releasing prayer and as he watched, a young boy appeared before them.

Gail was smiling at him, a look of pure wonder on her face as the boy smiled, waved, and then dissipated in a flash of light.

I need to tell you something, Alice spoke in his mind. *I can't leave the house.*

"It's too dangerous," Jesse shouted.

You have to hear this.

Jesse was slowing, he didn't feel it, but he could see it in the look of panic that crossed Gail's face. She was reaching out to him, screaming, begging, but he had to go back. He didn't know why, but he knew it was the right thing to do. Shaking his head, he mouthed the words *I'm sorry* before turning and racing back to the burning building.

Gail's screams rang in his ears as he raced back to the house.

The flames were leaping out of the window now, and the roof looked ready to collapse. Logically, he knew this was the wrong thing to do, but he couldn't stop his legs, and he ran into the smoke and flames.

As he disappeared from view, a boom rocketed across the night, and the house became an inferno.

As the fireball died down the house collapsed in on itself leaving four ragged children in the ashes, but no sign of Jesse.

Gail let out a wail of grief and dropped to her knees.

CHAPTER 28

*J*esse could hear Gail scream, and still, he ran toward the fire. The black smoke hid the house from his view and clogged his lungs. It burned his eyes, and as he walked away from Gail and safety, the heat was becoming unbearable. *What was he doing?*

I just need a moment," Alice spoke in his head.

"Okay," the word came from him calmly, despite his panic, and then the air was clear. He could see and breathe, and he appeared to be within a bubble within the fire. Flames and smoke swirled and flared just inches from his face, but he was safe... for now.

I can hold you safe for just a moment. Others are here to help me.

Jesse nodded and then he saw them. The circle was surrounded by spirits, all dressed in white. They were people he didn't know, but he could feel their goodness, and he knew he was in no danger.

"Gail will be afraid, please don't take too long," Jesse said.

I want to help Rosie, Alice said.

"I understand but how?"

I have learned a lot since I crossed. I could have gone to peace, but I felt a debt needed paying. I have aligned with those who have been here longer. She looked around the circle, and the spirits nodded their heads in approval.

They know the ones with dark souls. They are good at whispering in their ears and pointing them to the way they want. If you point the champion to the man called Philip Jackson, then he will find the evidence you need.

"I don't understand," Jesse said. "Are you martyring this man to free Rosie?" Though he desperately wanted to free Rosie, he didn't know if he could put someone else in jail just because they had a bad soul.

Alice lowered her eyes and blushed slightly. Such a gesture from the young ghost almost broke Jesse's heart. She was good and honest and pure. He couldn't believe that she would do such a thing.

Alice raised her eyes and smiled. *The old ones choose wisely. This man is known to your police as one who hurts children. He travels to all the lonely places, and there he commits acts so gross that we know he will never find peace. However, he's clever and has not been caught. In three weeks' time, he has another trip planned and an innocent life he wishes to extinguish.*

We want to help Rosie, but there are others we want to protect. Other lives we want to save. Tell the champion to look at the recording from the streets on the night of Mary's death. He will see enough for your police to get a warrant and they will find what they need.

"Recording?" Jesse asked.

The box near the shop that records time.

Jesse shook his head, he did not understand.

Alice looked at the spirits around the circle. He could see her frustration. Then she held up her hands and mimicked an old-fashioned wind-up film camera.

"Of course, the CCTV." Jesse wasn't sure how Paul would do this, but he knew the solicitor would find a way. "I have to go now," Jesse said, "but thank you for doing this. Now rest in peace."

Alice smiled, and the spirits started to move toward him. For a second, panic gripped onto his heart, but then he noticed they were all moving. They were shepherding him out of the fire. After a few feet, Alice faded, disappearing with a slight wave and a sweet smile. Then the further he got from the house the less of them were around him. Once they were all gone, he could see out of the smoke, and he ran straight into Gail's arms.

CHAPTER 29

*J*esse held Gail's hand as they watched the house burn down. Timbers fell, and then the walls crashed in, producing a great leap of flames into the air.

Jack sat on the damp grass. He refused to leave, as they all did. There was something about the sight that just pulled in the eyes. At times, the flames had appeared alive. Like a ferocious beast that leaped out to get them. It was so real that many times during the night they had moved back. But now it was over. The house was just a pile of smoldering rubble. Or at least that was what they hoped.

"Can you feel anything?" Jesse asked Gail.

She leaned against his shoulder, and the warmth of her took away the aches and pain.

"No. After we released those last few children I have felt nothing."

"Good."

Jesse thought back. Once he appeared from the flames, he found Shelly, Gail, and Jack performing an exorcism on the last remaining adult ghost. They left in darkness screaming out their torment. Their faces contorted as they tried to hang onto this plane. It was no use, their power was gone and soon, so where they.

Sending them back had cleansed the place. The air was lighter, easier to breathe and a great sense of calm, of anticipation, descended upon them all.

Then he had joined in while they sent the four ragged children to peace. It was such an amazing sight that he still felt the wonder of each one. How their faces changed from despair to joy and how they faded away leaving, just a flash of light before they were gone.

They were all warmed, fortified by the sight, and they knew that they would never be the same again.

Stacey had appeared shortly after Jesse. Now she was deep in conversation with her sister. Jesse could see that the two had a special connection and he wondered what to do about Stacey. His instincts, his training from his grandparents, told him that he should send her to peace... but his gut said let it be. Maybe he could give them a bit of time together. He would just have to explain to Shelly that if she stayed too long, then Stacey would change.

There was one more thing he needed to do, one reason he was still waiting, despite their fatigue — Nick. The priest had been sent away sometime during the battle, and so far, he hadn't returned. Jesse owed him his peace, and he would wait as long as was needed to see that he got it. Part of him wanted to get Jack to the hospital, though he had no idea what to tell them. Stacey and Jack had both assured him that he was in no danger. Uncomfortable, scared, but he would live, he would heal.

Jesse glanced at him. Despite the loose skin hanging around his jaw and the stretch marks on his cheeks, he looked happy. Jesse understood that. Up until today, he had believed in ghosts to help Shelly. Now he had seen that there was something else. Though he didn't know what, he could sense in on a primal level, it changed you. Jesse chuckled.

"What's so funny?" Gail asked.

"I was just thinking about Jack and what a paradigm-shift he's just had." He raised his eyebrows and then kissed her forehead.

"I remember it well." She winked. "Full on bowel emptying fear followed by the most profound peace I've ever known. Weird and kinda addictive."

"Yeah, I can see these two will be getting into all sorts of problems now."

Gail snuggled back on to his shoulder. "Maybe we can help them?"

Before Jesse could answer, he saw a shape walking toward them… a man, and for a moment his stomach clenched. Was it over?

The smoke cleared a little.

"Nick, it's so good to see you."

Jesse had the urge to pull the spirit into a hug, but he restrained himself.

"I'm sorry I had to leave," Nick said. "It looks like you managed without me."

"We did." He wanted to say more to explain how they couldn't have done it without Nick. How the priest had saved the children.

Nick smiled and nodded, and Jesse knew that he had heard his thoughts.

"They have gone to peace?" Nick asked.

"All of them. It was amazing." Jesse knew he was grinning like a loon. "Is... is it finally over?"

Nick turned and looked back at the smoldering ruins. "There is evil here, a darkness, a stain on the ground, and there always will be — however there is nothing to harness it — I pray it stays that way."

Jesse felt a curl of fear loop around his intestines. "Can we assure that?"

Nick turned back to them and smiled. "No one is here, no one comes here, and without death, the place is just a place."

Jesse felt a tug inside, and his throat tightened. He knew it was time. "I made you a promise, my friend. Do you wish me to keep it?"

Gail's hand tightened on his, and he heard her gulp. She would be fighting back the tears. Though this was a happy event, it meant that Nick would be gone and they would never see him again.

Nick turned again and surveyed all the land around them. For long moments he said nothing and then he turned back and nodded. "It is time."

Jesse nodded, but before he could say anything else, Nick had gone, and Jesse understood.

He crossed to Shelly, Jack, and Stacey. "We have something to do. It won't take long. Are you okay here?"

"We're fine," Jack said from his position on the floor.

Jesse nodded and kept his face neutral. Jack had a long way to go, but he could teach them both about protection, and more, if they wanted to continue with this.

Shelly looked afraid. "You're... well...y....y... you're not going to send Stacey away, are you?"

"No, I will leave the timing of that to you two. You have talent. Would you like to join us sometime?"

Shelly let out a shriek of delight and pulled them both into a hug.

"I'll take that as a yes," Jesse said, as they extracted themselves.

Go, Stacey said in their minds. *He is waiting, and it's his time.*

Jesse held her eyes for a moment. She understood that he would be watching her. Nick had stayed sane throughout his long vigil, but that was rare.

Stacey nodded.

It took Jesse and Gail just ten minutes to walk back through the woods to the little clearing and the grave. Nick was waiting.

"Thank you, my friend," Jesse said.

Nick nodded, and they could see tears in his eyes.

Gail ran to him and pulled him into a hug before pushing him to arm's length. "You are sure?"

He nodded.

Jesse pulled the crucifix from his pocket and handed it back. Nick took it and smiled, holding it to his chest.

Standing in a circle around the crumbled gravestone, they recited the releasing prayer together.

"In the Name of Jesus, we rebuke the spirit of Nickolas Aubrey."

Jesse stopped and turned to Gail. "Let me finish this."

She nodded.

Jesse reached out and took Nick's hands. They were cold, but he could feel them, and a slight tingle ran across the hairs of his hands.

"In the Name of Jesus, we rebuke the spirit of Nickolas Aubrey. A good man, a man who saved many and stayed true to God. Go to peace my friend, leave this place without manifestation."

The fingers in his hand were no longer solid. The sensation of cold increased and static raised the hair all up Jesse's arms.

"Go to a better place, a place of peace where He will greet you with the love and redemption you deserve."

The fingers were gone, and Jesse dropped his hands. Nick was fading, but there was a huge smile on his face.

"Know that you have found redemption and we will be forever grateful for your courage. Now leave this place according to His Holy Will."

Light surrounded Nick, and then it shrunk to a spot, and he was gone.

The crucifix dropped to the ground, and they heard the words, *For you. May it bring you peace and keep you safe.*

"OMG," Gail said. "That was beautiful, but you didn't use the real words."

Jesse laughed and put an arm around her shoulders. "It's the intention that counts, remember? I felt Nick deserved more."

"Yeah, now let's go home, I'm desperate for a pee."

Jesse laughed. "Me, too."

CHAPTER 30

Three Months Later

Jesse, Gail, and Amy sat in the courtroom waiting for the verdict. Behind them were Shelly and Jack. His face had shrunk back down to its normal size, but the bruising and stretch marks would take a little longer to fade. He smiled as Jesse looked back. The incident didn't seem to have curbed his enthusiasm.

Next to Shelly, Stacey sat completely still. Jesse was still thrilled that he could see her, for he knew most of the courtroom couldn't. That was probably for the best as she was struggling to be here and was translucent, occasionally fading away completely.

Stacey nodded when she caught his eye and Jesse gave her the thumbs-up. He had a good feeling about this, and as Stacey was part of the reason why they were here, he wanted her to feel good.

Jesse turned back to the front as the jury filed back into the courtroom.

Paul Simmonds sat next to Rosie, as calm as ever. It had been a tense three months since they had escaped RedRise House, but he still looked as if he was simply waiting for afternoon tea. Despite that, a lot had happened, and these next few minutes would decide the rest of Rosie's life.

Jesse held his breath. Gail squeezed his hand, as he thought back over how they got here.

After they escaped from RedRise House, they had sought Out Rosie's lawyer, Paul Simmons. Paul had listened to their story and said that he would see what he could do. It didn't take him long to find an officer who had an interest in Phillip Jackson.

Phillip was well known as the worst type of pedophile. His nickname was Teflon; nothing would stick to him. Apparently, he wore gloves and a hair net wherever he went and was meticulous to make sure he never left any trace evidence.

Paul asked around and soon found a Detective, John Evans, who was prepared to look at the CCTV. When they reviewed it, Phillip was definitely lurking. There he was on the spotty footage, across the street from Rosie, skulking in the shadows. Paul suspected he was waiting for children to come to the shop, but it didn't matter. They had enough for a warrant.

When the police raided Jackson's house, they found a blood-soaked shirt and a diary that was full of his fantasies. It told of how he forced Rosie to do as he said. He wrote extensively of her terror, of him holding a knife to her throat, and of how he committed the murders, but that she was just there as a scapegoat. How he forced her to cover herself in blood and told her that he would kill her and all her friends if she spoke of it.

The more they searched, the worse it became. His internet scrubber had not been working, and all the sites he had visited in the last few weeks were there to view. That was enough to put him away for a long time. As they were about to leave, a book fell off a shelf, and a receipt for a necklace fell out. It was for a pink crystal rose on a gold chain, and it had been found on the third victim. They had enough to convict and were lucky that they acted when they did, as they also found a one-way ticket to Bangladesh.

Jesse remembered the words the young spirit spoke to him, *He travels to all the lonely places... an innocent life he wishes to extinguish.*

It had taken a month and a half to get to that stage, and then the police had decided there was enough evidence to bring Rosie to a court of appeal. Paul and Jesse had spent a long time with her, coaching, and helping her, and they had finally got to this decision.

The trial had taken just a few weeks, and now they were waiting for the verdict. Jesse looked around and smiled at Jack, Shelly, and Stacey, for without them, they would never be here. He whispered a thank you to them.

Shelly nodded her head, her mousy brown ponytail swung across her shoulders. This was where it all started for her, just a few months before she had been sitting here watching the first trial. Then she had taken it upon herself to do something. Jesse couldn't thank her enough.

Jesse looked back to the court as he heard the jury walk back in and take their seats. His breath was held, and he felt as if the whole room held theirs with him. It took them all a long time to settle down, and Jesse wanted to scream at them to get it over with. He couldn't imagine how Rosie must feel, yet she looked so calm.

The clerk of the court faced the jury. "Will the jury please rise." He turned to Rosie. "Will the defendant also please rise and face the jury."

Wood scraped on the hard floor, and the sound of people standing echoed around the cavernous room. Rosie stood easily, and Paul stood next to her. The smile on his face was calm and assured.

"Mr. Foreman, has your jury agreed upon your verdicts?"

A sharply dressed woman in her early thirties with long brown hair held an envelope in her hand. "We have." She passed the envelope to the clerk who took it to the judge. The only sound was of the clerk's feet on the wooden floor, slap, slap, slapping as he walked back to the jury.

"What say you, Ms. Forman, as to complaint number 5879644, wherein the defendant is charged with three counts of manslaughter on the grounds of diminished responsibility? Is she guilty or not guilty?"

"Not guilty."

Jesse let out his breath in a great whoosh, and he heard the screams of joy that echoed through the courtroom.

Shelly was on her feet and dancing around. Some of the relatives were celebrating with her, which amazed Jesse. She had done what she said she would, albeit leaving out the bits about spirits. She had explained to them that Rosie was a victim and they had gotten behind her and helped bring them to this day.

Gail pulled Jesse into her arms. "I can't believe today," she whispered in his ear. "I think this is one of the best days yet."

Jesse kissed her neck. "I couldn't agree more."

Amy had run down to the front of the courtroom and was hugging Rosie, as half of the room had tears in their eyes.

Jesse pulled back and looked across at Paul. They shared a glance, and Jesse noticed that Paul looked a little happier than normal. Maybe seeing that spirits could do some good had helped him a little.

Jesse pulled Gail back into his arms. "Now everyone is free, why don't we set a date?"

"A date?" Gail asked, but he could see from the cheeky twinkle in her eyes that she knew what he meant.

"A date for our wedding. I want everyone here today to come."

Gail laughed. "Not the prosecutor, I hope."

"Oh, you are so annoying, you know what I mean. Marry me, just tell me when."

Gail rolled her eyes at him and then gave him her cutest smile. He knew it, she had been thinking the same thing.

"Thursday, June 7th."

"Thursday... wait... how come you came up with that so quickly?"

Gail kissed him and then pulled away. "Thursdays are cheaper, and June 7th is Sylvia's birthday. It gives us plenty of time to prepare and time to get all these friends organized. What do you say?"

"I can't wait. Now let's go join in the celebrations. We can tell them in a couple of weeks. Today is all for Rosie."

* * *

THE FOLLOWING NIGHT, a fox trotted out of the woods around RedRise House. A smell, something burned, drew it to a place it would not normally come. The moon shone down over the ruins, and the fox skirted around, sniffing and searching for something to eat. It had been a hard year, and food was scarce. There was something enticing in the rubble, but something held it back.

Slowly it trotted around the edges of the destruction. There was meat in the ruins, something burned, but delicious. Sniffing the air, tasting the wind, it searched for the source to no avail.

The wreckage still smoldered all this time after the fire, and if it weren't starving, the fox would never come this close. Cautious, it weaved in and out of the bushes, always watching for danger.

Then it found the source and padded across the hot remains to snatch a morsel of meat. It was ripe and nutritious, but not a taste it had experienced before. Gulping down the first mouthful, it snatched and tore off another.

A tree broke behind it, and the fox turned. Fear caused a whimper to leave its throat. Something lurked in the darkness, something that made it forget the food and run back into the woods as fast as its legs would carry it.

Maybe there was *still* something lurking at RedRise House.

* * *

IF YOU MISSED the first book in this amazing series The Ghosts of RedRise House The Sacrifice get it now on SALE at 0.99 for a limited time only http://a-fwd.to/7APCHD3

To find out when my next book is available join my newsletter now http://eepurl.com/cGdNvX

THE HAUNTING OF OLDFIELD DRIVE
– PREVIEW

Called From Beyond

6th July, 2018

Country Road,

Yorkshire

England

11:59 p.m.

Mark stared out through the windscreen at the dark and twisty road ahead. The long drive back to civilization dulled his senses and the warm car tempted him with sleep. He stifled a yawn and shook his head to fight the fatigue. "We probably should have stayed the night." Taking his eyes off the road, he turned to face Alissa.

Her feet were curled up on the seat next to her, her eyes almost closed. "Mmm, probably. It was good to see them again," she said, pushing her long blonde hair back from her face.

He loved to see it when it fell in whispers across her pale skin, so fine and silky to the touch. Right now, he just wanted them back in the hotel so he could hold her. These bleak and lonely roads were no place for a couple of city kids like them, and he couldn't wait to get back to the noise and bustle of Leeds.

They had booked a room at a hotel in one of the small villages—he had hoped to make it a bit of a romantic night as well as a reunion—but now he wished they hadn't. Maybe he should have taken her away somewhere special, not just down the road from their house?

"It *was* good," he said, pulling his eyes back to the road. "They both looked so healthy. And the food? Mmmm. Amazing."

"Don't I know it." Alissa's bright smile contrasted with the dreamy quality her eyes still held. "That stroganoff was so creamy and delicious. I think that's why I'm so sleepy. I'm way too full."

Mark laughed. "Or perhaps a few too many glasses of red wine?"

"You're jealous because tonight was your turn to drive." She stuck her tongue out and her green eyes danced with laughter.

"Funny, that." He tried to put a stern expression on his face. "It's always your turn to drive on the way there and mine to drive back."

"Yeah, I like the way that works out." She snorted a giggle and closed her eyes again. "Perfect, if you ask me."

Mark laughed and turned back to the road. Fatigue was like a heavy blanket and his eyes just wanted to close. He quickly rubbed a hand through his short brown hair. Though he was no longer enlisted, he never let his hair grow more than a finger. He unwound the window and let a cool breeze travel across his scalp. The fresh draft was much more invigorating than the cold air from the blowers. Right now, he needed something to bring back his concentration. At least another twelve miles laid between them and anything that even remotely resembled an A road.

"Do you think they made the right decision?" Alissa asked.

"You mean moving out here?"

"Yeah, it's a long way from London."

Mark thought about it. He missed their friends so he wanted to say no, then he thought about how much they'd laughed and smiled tonight. "We made the move for your job, what was it... three years ago now?"

"We moved to a city."

"Leeds is a big city but it's not London and you adapted."

Alissa grumbled. "I know, but right out in the country and into that old rundown house?"

"It looked pretty nice to me. They're happy there and that's all that counts, right?" It hit him hard that he wanted things to change. That she wanted more from the relationship was no secret and finally, he understood. He turned to look at her.

That pretty smile he loved so much mocked him just a little. She was a picture to behold with perfect skin, a heart-shaped face, and the biggest green eyes you ever did see. A splattering of freckles danced across her nose and more tiptoed down her arms.

Sometimes he tried to count them when she was asleep.

They had been engaged for a year now, but when he proposed, it had simply been a stop gap for him—a way to appease her—and he never intended the engagement as a prelude to marriage. That stank!

She gave everything to him, was always generous and loving. His best friend.

How could he treat her like that? He wanted to marry her, but this was the wrong time to set the date. He had to make it more romantic.

She deserved that.

"Keep your eyes on the road," she gently admonished.

Nodding, he turned back. The headlights hardly cut through the gloom and he eased up on the accelerator, slowing the car just a touch. The beams of light shone into the ether as they topped a brow, and then dropped to the tarmac as they began to descend. The dark and twisted trees lining the road on their right sucked the light from the moon. To their left, the ground sloped alarmingly away and more trees, along with the occasional sheep, dotted the grassland. He hated the fact that sheep were on the road. Where were the fences? Surely farm animals were supposed to be fenced in for safety?

"Penny for them?" she said, bringing him back to the moment and the feelings that had snuck up on him.

"Why don't we stay another night? We could come for a walk

on the moors, have a nice romantic meal, and then just chill a little."

Alissa laughed, a silky sound that stroked down his nerves and filled him with love. "When I look out the window all I can hear is, *Stay on the road—keep clear of the moors.*'"

Mark laughed. What other woman would get his favorite film? An old one, for sure, but still the best. "Maybe we could find a pub called the Slaughtered Lamb?"

Alissa chuckled. "No, that would be too freaky."

Green eyes opened wide, staring, as her mouth dropped open.

"Mark!" her voice was high pitched and cut through the joy like a knife through silk.

The world slowed as he turned his head back to the road.

The headlights barely penetrated the soft mist in front of them, but he clearly saw a woman standing there. A white dress fluttered around her thin frame. Her face seemed carved in granite.

Frozen in an eternal scream.

Mark yanked on the steering wheel and jerked the car to the left. He tensed, waiting for the crunch as steel hit flesh and broke bones—a sound he knew well—and a memory of war flashed into his mind. Broken flesh. Blood. A world of fear and pain.

Pulling himself from the nightmare of his past, he yanked harder on the wheel and trusted his reactions were good. The car turned instantly. The force pushed him into the seat but it shouldn't have been quick enough to miss the woman.

He tensed for the crunch but it never came, just a flutter of white whipped across the windscreen.

They left the road and tore across the grass. Like a turbo powered shopping trolley, they careered down the hill, out of control.

Trees loomed out of the black as the headlights and power went out. The car plunged into darkness. The engine had died but, nevertheless, they hurtled on down the hill. Mark pulled left and right, avoiding a sheep then a tree. Everything lurched out of the dark and was on them so soon. His right foot pressed hard on the brakes, but nothing happened. Stamping his foot down on the clutch, he pushed the gear lever into first. The car should have slowed considerably, had to slow, but it didn't. Before he could do anything else, another tree loomed out of the darkness and engulfed them.

This time, the crunch was bone wrenching as they ground to a halt. He instinctively reached out to his left to steady Alissa, but was too late. They both flew forward until they hit their seatbelts.

Another crunch and breaking glass showered him as the car finally shuddered to a halt.

In the pitch black, Mark's ears rang and his chest hurt. His training kicked in and he assessed the situation and his own injuries. Nothing but cuts and bruises. His neck was jarred and his knees had impacted with the steering column. They ached like hell, but the seat belt had saved him from worse injuries.

The car was stable for now, but how was Alissa? Leaves cut out the moon and he could only make out shapes. As his eyes adjusted to the dark, he searched for her and his phone. The seat belt was in the way. He couldn't reach the clasp. Fighting down terror, he methodically searched for the catch.

Alissa! The thought of her injured threatened to drive him to panic, but that wouldn't help. Although his chest ached from the seatbelt strain, he managed to cough out, "Babe, are you okay?" So far, he couldn't hear her moving but it could just be that the compression from the bang had affected his ears. Many a shell blast had given him a permanent ringing, but now they were almost screaming at him. Why was it so dark? Why had the lights gone out? He didn't know but they had no time to worry about that now. They had to get out of the car.

At last, he managed to free the seat belt and tipped forward. Reaching for his phone, he pulled it from his pocket and shook it twice. The torch light lit up and he almost let out a wail of grief.

Alissa was looking at him. Her eyes were glassy. Not the glassy darkness of death. This was the shine of shock, of trauma. He had to act quickly.

"Hey, baby, how are you?" He spoke gently but as matter of factly as he could.

Her eyelashes fluttered. She was awake and aware. That was good. For a moment, the woman on the road came to mind, but he pushed the thought away. They had missed her, but it didn't matter. Even if he had hit her, he could do nothing about it now. *Deal with what you can.* That was what his training had taught him. *Don't go looking for more trouble.* Once he had gotten Alissa out of danger, he would search for the woman.

He checked Alissa for injuries and a groan nearly escaped him as panic threatened to overwhelm.

She was leaning back against the seat. Her face looked fine, just pale, but that wasn't what scared him so.

A tree branch jutted out of her left shoulder. The gnarled and green wood had pierced straight through her light green top, through flesh, blood, and sinew, and into the car seat.

Think!

For a moment, he grasped the branch sticking out from her shoulder.

Alissa let out a groan of anguish and he pulled his hand away.

Blood was leaking from the wound, just a trickle. If he pulled the branch clear, he would be able to move her from the car but the wound would bleed much more quickly. If she had severed an artery, she would be dead before he could do anything to stop it.

First aid kit!

He sprang from the car and battled the branches of an oak tree. They crumbled easily with each strike. The old and weary tree could topple onto the car any second now. Alissa would be crushed. Each groan and creak of the limbs surrounding him forced a bead of sweat onto his forehead.

He pulled up the coordinates of where they were on his phone, then dialed for an ambulance as he moved around to the back of the car.

Mark popped the boot and immediately spotted the first aid kit strapped against the wheel arch.

"Emergency services, which service please?"

"Ambulance," he said as he grabbed the kit. Alissa's door was buried deep beneath unstable branches. He didn't want to waste time digging her out or risk disturbing the hovering tree, so he went back to the driver's side.

With the phone clamped between his neck and shoulder, he opened the kit and crawled back into the car.

What now!?

"Help me?" Alissa pleaded. On her cheeks, the glint of tears mocked his indecisiveness.

"I'm here, baby. You'll be out of here any minute."

"Ambulance, what's your emergency?"

Mark explained as he packed around the wound with gauze.

"The ambulance is on the way. You need to leave her where she is and go back to the road to help guide the driver to the right spot," the operator told him.

Mark recognized the tone, designed to keep him calm and busy. For a moment, he thought about it. But he couldn't leave her. The tree groaned above him, how long would it hold? Would he get her out before it came crashing down?

Alissa's breathing was ragged now. Panicked.

Hearing her in such pain tore out his heart.

"I can't leave her and I have military training. Just get to these coordinates," he said and dropped the phone back into his pocket.

"You have to get me out of here." Alissa grabbed hold of his hand.

Her grip was weak, her fingers cold.

"I will, baby, but you must be patient."

Leaves rustled overhead and a branch fell, bouncing off the top of the car. They were out of time. He needed to get her out of there, but he'd have to pull the branch from her shoulder to do so. The angle was wrong from the driver's seat. If he did it from here, he would tear open her wound. If he did that, he doubted he'd be able to stop the bleeding in time.

She'd bleed out in his arms.

If he could get in through the passenger door, then it would be a cleaner jerk. The branch would come out at the same angle as it had entered her shoulder and he could staunch the flow more easily. If he could get her from the car, he could possibly even tie off the artery.

"Just hold still a moment," he said and pulled her fingers from his.

Panic gave her strength. Despite her small size, she clung on so desperately that he struggled to free his hand.

"I will just be a moment," he whispered against her ear, then gently kissed her hair. The blonde tresses were no longer silky but wet with blood. Had she hurt her head?

He couldn't worry about it now, so he left the car and fought his way to the front and through the fallen tree. A large branch was wedged against the door, and he kicked at it to break it free. The tree above them shuddered and rained down sticks and smaller branches. Something groaned and cracked, and still the door was wedged tight. He kicked at the branch with all his might, knowing he had a choice between time and force. Too much time and the tree might collapse on top of them, too much force and he might hasten that outcome. His foot hit the branch and it slid across the door. The tortured metal screamed but the branch fell away.

He pulled on her door, but the impact had bent the metal. His breathing was ragged, and the fear inside him fought like a wild horse for freedom but he reined it in. Feeling around the door, he found the dent and then kicked the panel to clear the frame.

Alissa let out a scream of pain.

Mark felt as if he had been stabbed in the gut, but he had to keep going. Grasping hold of the door, he pulled with all he had. For a moment, nothing happened and his muscles protested at the effort. Gradually, his eyes adjusted to the darkness as he worked to free the door.

With one last gargantuan effort, he hauled the door open as far as it would go.

Alissa's eyes were drawn down, her mouth grimacing in pain. That was a good sign. If she could feel, then she hadn't gone into shock yet and there was hope.

He fought around the door. Before he could lean into the car, a ripping sound dragged his gaze upward. A thick branch tore free from the trunk and fell down, and down. The massive limb smashed through the windscreen and slammed into Alissa's face with a dull thunk.

As warm wet splashed his face, Mark screamed, certain he'd never be able to stop.

* * *

Find out what mistakes Mark makes by reading The Haunting of Oldfield Drive - Called From Beyond A Woman in White Ghost Story FREE on Kindle Unlimited http://a-fwd.to/1w2qbGw

THE HAUNTING OF SEAFIELD
HOUSE – PREVIEW.

30th June 1901

Seafield House.

Barton Flats,

Yorkshire.

England.

1. am.

Jenny Thornton sucked in a tortured breath and hunkered down behind the curtains. The coarse material seemed to stick to her face, to cling there as if holding her down. Fighting back the thought and the panic it engendered she crouched even lower and tried to stop the shaking of her knees, to still the panting of her breath. It was imperative that she did not breathe too loudly, that she kept quiet and still. If she was to survive with just a beating, then she knew she must hide. Tonight he was worse than she had ever seen him before. Somehow, tonight was different, she could feel it in the air.

Footsteps approached on the landing. They were easy to hear through the door and seemed to mock her as they approached. Each step was like another punch to her stomach, and she could feel them reverberating through her bruises. Why had she not fled the house?

As if in answer, lightening flashed across the sky and lit up the sparsely furnished room. There was nothing between her and the door. A dresser to her right provided no shelter for an adult yet her eyes were drawn to the door on its front. It did not move but stood slightly ajar. Inside, her precious Alice would keep quiet. They had played this game before, and the child knew that she must never come out when Daddy was angry. When he was shouting. Would it be enough to keep her safe? Why had Jenny chosen this room? Before she could think, thunder boomed across the sky and she let out a yelp.

Tears were running down her face, had he heard her? It seemed unlikely that he could hear such a noise over the thunder and yet the footsteps had stopped. *Oh my, he was coming back.* Jenny tried to make herself smaller and to shrink into the thick velvet curtains, but there was nowhere else to go.

If only she had listened to her father, if only she had told him about Alice. For a moment, all was quiet, she could hear the house creak and settle as the storm raged outside. The fire would have burned low, and soon the house would be cold. This was the least of her problems. Maybe she should leave the room and lead Abe away from their daughter. Maybe it was her best choice. Their best choice.

Lightning flashed across the sky and filled the room with shadows. Jenny let out a scream for he was already there. A face like an overstuffed turkey loomed out of the darkness, and a hand grabbed onto her dress. Jenny was hauled off her feet and thrown across the room. Her neck hit the top of the dresser, and she slumped to the floor next to the door. How she wanted to warn Alice to stay quiet, to stay inside but she could not make a sound. There was no pain, no feeling and yet she knew that she was broken. Something had snapped when she hit the cabinet, and somehow she knew it could never be fixed. That it was over for her. In her mind, she prayed that her daughter, the child who had become her daughter, would be safe just before a distended hand reached out and grabbed her around the neck. There was no feeling just a strange burning in her lungs. The fact that she did not fight seemed to make him angrier and she was picked up and thrown again.

As she hit the window, she heard the glass shatter, but she did not feel the impact. Did not feel anything. Suddenly, the realization hit her and she wanted to scream, to wail out the injustice of it but her mouth would not move. Then he was bending over her.

"Beg for your life, woman," Abe Thornton shouted and sprayed her with spittle.

Jenny tried to open her mouth, not to beg for her own life but to beg for that of her daughter's. She wanted to ask him to tell others about the child they had always kept a secret, the one that he had denied. To admit that they had a daughter and maybe to let the child go to her grandparents. Only her mouth would not move, and no sound came from her throat.

She could see the red fury in his eyes, could feel the pressure building up inside of him and yet she could not even blink in defense. This was it, the end, and for a moment, she welcomed the release. Then she thought of Alice, alone in that cupboard for so long. Now, who would visit her, who would look after her? There was no one, and she knew she could never leave her child.

Abe grabbed her by the front of her dress and lifted her high above his head. The anger was like a living beast inside him, and he shook her like she was nothing but a rag doll. Then with a scream of rage, he threw her. This time she saw the curtains flick against her face and then there was nothing but air.

The night was dark, rain streamed down, and she fell with it. Alongside it she fell, tumbling down into the darkness. In her mind she wheeled her arms, in her mind she screamed out the injustice, but she never moved, never made a sound.

Instead, she just plummeted toward the earth.

Lightning flashed just before she hit the ground. It lit up the jagged rocks at the base of the house, lit up the fate that awaited her and then it was dark. Jenny was overwhelmed with fear and panic, but there was no time to react, even if she could. Jenny smashed into the rocks with a hard thump and then a squelch, but she did not feel a thing.

"Alice, I will come back for you," she said in her mind. Then it was dark, it was cold, and there was nothing.

Read The Haunting of Seafield House now just 0.99 or FREE on Kindle Unlimited.

More Books from Caroline Clark

Get two FREE short stories and never miss a book. Subscribe to Caroline Clark's newsletter for new release announcements and occasional free content: http://eepurl.com/cGdNvX

2 Short Stories Free

Click Here to Download

ALSO BY CAROLINE CLARK

The Spirit Guide Series:

The Haunting of Seafield House - Gail wants to create some memories – if she survives the night in Seafield House it is something she will never forget.

The Haunting on the Hillside - Called From Beyond – The Spirit Guide - A Woman in White Ghost Story. A non-believer, a terrible accident, a stupid mistake. Is Mark going mad or was his girlfriend Called from Beyond?

The Hauntiong of Oldfield Drive - DarkMan Alone in the dark, Margie must face unimaginable terror. Is this thing that haunts her nights a ghost or is it something worse?

The Ghosts of RedRise House Series:

The Sacrifice Dark things happened in RedRise House. Acts so bad they left a stain on the soul of the building. Now something is lurking there... waiting... dare you enter this most haunted house?

The Battle Within - The Ghosts of RedRise House have escaped. Something evil is stalking the city and only Rosie stands between it and a chain of misery and death.

Suffer the Children – Two young ghost hunters find themselves in a house that will not let them leave.

Standalone Books

The Haunting of Brynlee House Based on a real haunted house - Brynlee House has a past, a secret, it is one that would be best left buried.

The Haunting of Shadow Hill House A move for a better future becomes a race against the past. Something dark lurks in Shadow Hill House and it is waiting.

Want Books for FREE before they hit Amazon?

Would like to become part of Caroline's advanced reader team?

We are looking for a few select people who love Caroline's books.

If accepted will receive a free copy of each book before it is released.

We will ask that you share the book on your social media once it is released and give us any feedback on the book.

You will also get the chance to interact with Caroline and make suggestions for improvements to books as well as for future books.

This is an exciting opportunity for anyone who love's the author's work. Click here to find out more details

Caroline Clark

Find all my books here:

USA http://amzn.to/2yYL9Pz

UK http://amzn.to/2z0W1MH

ABOUT THE AUTHOR

Want Books for FREE before they hit Amazon?

Would like to become part of Caroline's advanced reader team?

We are looking for a few select people who love Caroline's books.

If accepted will receive a free copy of each book before it is released.

We will ask that you share the book on your social media once it is released and give us any feedback on the book.

You will also get the chance to interact with Caroline and make suggestions for improvements to books as well as for future books.

This is an exciting opportunity for anyone who love's the author's work. Click <u>here</u> to find out more details.

Caroline Clark is a British author who has always loved the macabre, the spooky, and anything that goes bump in the night.

She was brought up on stories from James Herbert, Shaun Hutson, Stephen King and more recently Darcy Coates, and Ron Ripley. Even at school she was always living in her stories and was often asked to read them out in front of the class, though her teachers did not always appreciate her more sinister tales.

Now she spends her time researching haunted houses or imagining what must go on inside them. These tales then get written up and become her books.

Caroline is married and lives in Yorkshire with her husband and their three boxer dogs. Of course one of them is called Spooky.

You can contact Caroline via her facebook page: https://www.facebook.com/CarolineClarkAuthor/

Via her newsletter: http://eepurl.com/cGdNvX

Or her website http://CazClark.com

She loves to hear from her readers.

I am also a member of the haunted house collective.
Why not discover great new authors like me?
Enter your email address to get weekly newsletters of hot
new haunted house books:
http://.hauntedhousebooks.info

UNTITLED

36884452R00160

Printed in Great Britain
by Amazon